THE ALCHEMISTS OF ARCHANGEL

ARCHANGEL REVOLUTION BOOK 2

TINA HOLLAND

The Alchemists of Archangel

By Tina Holland

❀ Created with Vellum

DEDICATION & ACKNOWLEGEMENTS

This book is dedicated to my daughter, Kyra, who is a biomolecular engineer and whose smarty-pants skillset inspired pieces of my heroine, Abigal Phelan.

I'd like to thank my writing groups who have supported me along the way, including The Founders Group, F-M Word Weavers, Writer Zen Garden, Moorhead Friends Writing Group, and the BisMan Writers Guild.

Thanks once again to my readers. I love hearing from you and am so glad that you all seem to appreciate this world I've created. Your Support helps each manuscript get to "THE END".

Cover Artist: Valerie Tibbs, Tibbs Design

Editor: Daniel Engelke

Format and Cover Wrap: J. Scott Coatsworth, Other Worlds Ink

CHAPTER ONE

Alchemia, New Archangel (Russian Settlement)
November 1, 1869

"Ouch!" Abigail Phelan cried out at the needle-sharp pain below her navel. She jumped back. The sweeping motion of the heavy silk around her waist held such momentum she nearly toppled off the dressmaker's box.

"Hold still." Emma Flannigan righted her, before placing more pins around the skirt.

"With less than a week away, you'll endure some torture. Why your father scheduled such a late fitting, I'll never know." Emma scolded Abigail. She'd finished the row of torturous pins around Abbie's waist and now began to fold the blue fabric under at the bottom.

Abigail kept her mouth shut. There was no reason to tell the dressmaker she was the cause for the late appointment. At four and twenty, she should handle her schedule but was content to let her father's secretary handle all mundane arrangements. She was conducting breakthrough research in her labs and didn't have time to acquire a new wardrobe, let alone a gown for the ball her father was hosting. She doubted Laurel would even care what people wore to the homecoming ball Professor Phelan was holding in honor of Doctor Benjamin and Laurel Gunn settling in Archangel.

"Will you be in attendance?" Abigail asked.

"With so few females in Archangel, of course," Emma replied.

Abigail narrowed her eyes.

"Don't be concerned, Abbie. Your father is not so rude. He invited all eligible single females including the day wives."

Day wives were nothing more than prostitutes. The Holy Alliance foothold in Archangel had strict laws against prostitution. Ever the enterprising institutions, brothels coined the phrase day-wife. Women were contracted rather than married because there were very small numbers of them. A day wife was contracted for a day. They were housed by a benefactor, and each house was run by a lawyer who handled all the contracts.

"All the benefactor houses were chosen?" Abbie couldn't imagine her father inviting all the houses, as there were a great many he didn't like.

"He invited Monique's house."

"Monique's Mail Order Brides?" Monique hardly ran a bordello. She ran a house near the train tracks where men could contract life brides. The only catch was women picked their husbands, and after a year the marriage could be annulled if no children were born and the wife didn't find the man agreeable. The period was referred to as a hand contract.

"Yes." Emma chuckled huskily, "you should've seen your eyes widen at the thought of day wives entering your home."

"I wouldn't have minded." She shrugged and added, "Papa hates lawyers though. He has since lost the patent on his agricultural dirigible to The Alchemist Consortium. It was bad enough that protocol dictated he invite the Consortium owners."

"So, who is this Laurel Gunn? Is it true she was a courtesan?" Emma asked.

"Laurel's father was a missionary in India when my father was in the Corps of Royal Engineers. Despite Laurel being seven years older, we played well together, and her mother assisted in my education. I was at a loss when her mother died. Brenna Kavanaugh was the only maternal force in my life and I haven't seen Laurel since the day of the funeral."

"Surely, you've written to each other?"

"No. Papa and Sir Kavanaugh had a falling out following Mrs. Kavanaugh's death." Abigail was lost in thought, remembering the events as a five-year-old child.

"She missed her own mother's funeral, you bastard." Abigail watched as her father raised his hand in a fist as if prepared to strike Daniel Kavanaugh.

"Edmund, you have no idea what kind of abhorrent creature she is." Mr. Kavanaugh shoved Laurel behind him.

"Let me take her then and prove you wrong." Abigail watched as her Papa reached for young Laurel, but his hand was struck aside with such force by Daniel Kavanaugh he nearly toppled backward onto Abbie. She stopped him by pressing with all her weight against his leg.

After finding his balance, Edmund Phelan kneeled beside his daughter. "I'm sorry, poppet, are you all right?" He gingerly examined her small limbs and scanned her face for injury.

"I'm okay, Papa." She assured him. "Is Laurel coming with us to America?" Abbie looked past the round legs of Mr. Kavanaugh to Laurel whose head was lowered. Silent tears hit the sandstone floor.

"If her father will let her?" Papa raised his face, darkened by wind and sun, to stare hard at Mr. Kavanaugh.

"No, Edmund. No." Mr. Kavanaugh turned to leave, dragging poor Laurel behind him.

"Wait!" Abigail bolted towards Laurel.

Laurel stopped and yanked on her father's hand.

Mr. Kavanaugh released her. He crossed his arms and tapped his foot as if timing this pause in his departure.

"What is it?" Laurel asked, her eyes wet from tears, and a reddening face showing concern.

"I want you to have this." Abigail took a closed fist from her apron pocket and handed over her most prized possession, a tiny pearl ring on a chain that had belonged to her mother.

"This is your mother's," Laurel whispered, looking down at the precious jewelry in her hand. Her lips trembled, and her brown eyes threatened to start more waterworks.

"Don't you cry, child, or I will beat you until you have nothing left," Mr. Kavanaugh whispered.

"You don't have a mother anymore. At least I have a parent who loves me." Abbie knew her barb hit its mark when Daniel Kavanaugh turned on her.

"Did you ever think perhaps her heathen soul was undeserving of love, Abigail?" With the harsh statement, he grabbed hold of Laurel with renewed determination.

Laurel took three steps to each of his long strides to keep up.

"Poppet," her father's voice broke through the cold sinking into Abbie's limbs.

When she turned, he lifted her into his arms and held her close. "That was *very kind of you, thinking of Laurel. Never change. You remind me so much of your mother with your generosity." Tears filled his eyes.*

Abbie had watched as her only friend was taken away by a man with such cruelty he should never bear the name of father.

Emotion brought Abigail back to the present, "I never saw Laurel again. I'm hoping she'll stop by and pick a bird for her hat."

Emma looked up at Abbie with her own watery eyes. "I'm sure she will."

Changing the subject, Abbie spoke up, "I'm very curious about the man who stole Laurel's heart. Papa said he was a doctor. We hadn't heard from Laurel since she married him. Only recently did she reach out to Papa to tell him she and her husband, Doctor Gunn, would be settling in Archangel."

"Where are they going to live? Winter is fast approaching." Emma nodded at the frosted windows.

Abbie shrugged, "If nothing else, we have plenty of room here at the mansion."

"Will you house people the night of the ball?" Emma asked.

"I'm sure we will, we have in the past. Of course, many will want to show off their new steam animals and sleds. Those with money never stay. The miners will, they always do and usually carouse with Papa's cook, secretary, and the maids." Abbie shook her head with a smile, as she remembered the summer festival her father held when the miners reached a large vein of copper. The celebration had extended late into the early morning.

Emma smoothed the skirt down. "There, I think that will do nicely. What do you think?"

Abbie turned around to face the mirror. She liked the color but didn't know enough about fashion to ascertain if it suited her. "If you think it's fine, who am I to complain?"

"The customer I'm making the dress for," Emma answered, staring at her in the mirror.

"I like the color," Abbie said, unsure if she truly did.

"Let's try something else." Emma pinched the bridge of her nose. "Do you have a bird to go with the dress?" Emma asked.

Abbie looked at the silk dress again and the deep blue reminded her of a peacock. Although her peacock Norman was much too big to place on a hat, he shed feathers regularly, and she always kept the feathers to sell to conventional hat makers. "It reminds me of Norman. Perhaps some feathers in a hat?" Abbie pointed to her head.

"I have an idea. Turn around," Emma commanded.

Abbie did as she was told.

Emma went to her reticule and pulled out a pen and paper and began scribbling. Abbie watched fascinated as the process reminded her of when she solved a problem. After a few minutes, Emma approached her, unwinding the tape draped over her neck.

"Stand up straight." Emma handed her the drawing before stretching the tape across Abbie's bottom.

Abbie stared at the drawing of peacock feathers as a bustle on a blue skirt and one long peacock feather in a hat to match.

"I like this!" Abbie turned towards Emma.

"Look straight ahead." Emma pointed.

Once Emma finished measuring for the bustle, she stood in front of Abbie.

"I'm afraid I won't have this bustle done by the time of the ball," Emma sighed.

A few minutes ago, Abbie didn't care and now she couldn't hide her disappointment. "I have a bunch of Norm's feathers," she offered.

"I wasn't concerned about the feathers." Emma waved her off. "I was thinking I need to find the right material to back the feathers and the proper thread for the delicate quills. I'll have to order both. The skirt will be complete though."

Abbie's shoulders dropped along with her chin. What's the point?

"That will be fine Emma," Abbie said. She supposed she could wear the completed dress to the Free Miner's Melee.

"Wonderful!" Emma clapped her hands before gathering up her supplies to see her other clients. Abbie was left alone to change.

"I'll send the skirt to your shop," Abbie said before Emma closed the door.

Emma popped her head back in; "Send it to my caravan. I'll finish it faster. You can send the feathers over too."

The door clicked shut and Abigail stepped off the platform Emma left behind.

She changed with efficiency, not dwelling on the stupid dress. Once in her overalls, she set out to track Norm down for some of his precious feathers.

* * *

THE FOLLOWING AFTERNOON, Abigail was disturbed in her greenhouse by George, a retired miner who served as the household butler.

" 'Scuse me, Abbie," he ventured timidly.

"Yes, George?"

"There's a coach, what's arrived at the door." George ran his finger underneath his collar, the starch was probably uncomfortable. She often wondered why her father bothered with the uniforms. The suit was a nuisance to George as indicated by his loosened and sideways bowtie. "Your Pa told us there'd be a Doc and his wife, but there are more folks than what he done told us about."

"Laurel and her husband have arrived," Abbie said joyfully. She removed her gardening gloves and set them down before turning to find Trumbo tooting his trunk at her waist. She patted the brass pachyderm on his head. Unlike most of her father's brass animal creations created for transport, Trumbo's steam-powered head had been replaced with circuits and Teslatricity. He had gone from being a means of transport as a child to something more like a pet as she got older. "Do you want to meet my friend, Trumbo?"

He honked in response. His emerald eyes flashed.

"Lead on George." Abbie gestured towards the tunnel leading to the house.

George led the way through the short cavern, lined with volcanic rock. The Phelan's took advantage of the hot springs and built the conservatory atop one. New Archangel itself had tunnels running beneath the town. The tunnels allowed people to travel in the winter months without venturing out into the cold. Almost all tunnels are connected from the city to the mines.

They entered the house through the kitchen and made their way to the front parlor. Abbie halted and looked at where Laurel and the four others stood.

George turned back to comment to Abbie. "Told you there was a mess of 'em."

Trumbo held no such reservation as he plodded forward trumpeting his greeting and circling the small group.

"My, my look at you," Laurel leaned down and patted Trumbo on the head, "Trumbo?"

"Yes," Abbie answered, stepping forward. She wanted to run and hug Laurel but held back. The woman in front of her was grown, and though they were once friends, Laurel may not welcome personal overtures.

"He seems different." Laurel cocked her head to the side.

"Papa replaced his steam power with Teslatricity and he follows some basic commands," Abbie responded.

"Fascinating." A dark-skinned young man, not much older than Abbie, said as he came around to peer at Trumbo.

Laurel stood and reached an arm towards Abbie. "Abbie, come and meet my family."

Abbie stepped forward until Laurel captured her hand and squeezed it.

"My heart, don't cry." The man beside Laurel said.

"I assure you, husband, these are tears of joy." She smiled at the auburn-haired man.

"Abigail Phelan, this is my husband, Doctor Benjamin Gunn," Laurel said, releasing her hand.

"A pleasure to meet you, Miss Phelan." Doctor Gunn spoke, wrapping an arm around Laurel.

"The young man covering Trumbo with black ink fingerprints is my son, Moody Djinn."

Abbie thought it odd Laurel had a son not much older than she. Abbie figured she would hear more in detail later so she didn't press. Trumbo enjoyed the attention, flapping his ears, and tilting his head from side to side.

Moody stood, wiping his hands on his pants, before extending one to Abigail. "Sorry about that." He nodded to the fingerprints on Trumbo's head.

"It's alright. I'll have you help me polish his head, and then you can learn how he works if you like."

Trumbo apparently liked the idea, as he knocked Moody's hand with his trunk, an indicator to pay him some attention.

While Trumbo monopolized Moody's time, Laurel introduced Libby, her maid, and Omar, her manservant. Unlike George, Abbie was not intimidated by the group's size. She planned with the staff to see them settled.

Almost an hour later, she knocked on the room where she had placed Laurel and her husband.

"Come in," Laurel called.

Abbie opened the door to find Libby unpacking a valise and running items to the bureau and dresser. Omar stood guard by the door and towered over Abbie as she entered. Laurel and Ben turned from looking out the window.

"Enjoying the view?" Abbie asked.

"Yes. Doctor Gunn and I were just discussing building."

"Oh?"

"Who owns the land adjacent to you?" Laurel asked.

"The Alchemist Consortium and the Free Miners own most of the land. Papa bought his land from the Free Miners. As part of the arrangement, he agrees to provide every miner with tools of their trade. We have tunnels off the south side of our land."

"Are there any abandoned mines?" Doctor Gunn asked.

"I'm sure there are, but none surrounding our lands. Perhaps Papa can be of assistance. He's familiar with all the mines. You can ask him at dinner. I'm afraid I'm going to be getting my birds ready for the ball and all the ladies' hats." Abbie confessed as she rattled on.

"I must stop and view your lovely animals, perhaps bring Moody along," Laurel said.

"Moody seems fascinated with Trumbo. He's spent the afternoon in the kitchen commanding Trumbo to do various tasks. I think Trumbo enjoys the attention."

"But he's a machine." Doctor Gunn said.

"True, but he seems quite capable of learning, and the engineer, Sam Brownsmith who mounted the circuit board, was very talented. Sam programmed all the brass mules to haul rock and ore out for the free miners. The mules follow basic commands, perform weight calculations, and do purity tests on the ore samples. They are an upgrade from the Jumbos and other brass animals you'll see the night of the ball."

"There are more brass animals?" Doctor Gunn asked.

"Yes, but they are like the Jumbos my father built in India."

"The ones in Constantinople are much the same," Laurel stated before a smile spread over her face.

"What is it, my heart?" her husband asked.

"Wait until Raven sees all these animals. He is going to go absolutely mad." Laurel smiled at her husband.

Doctor Gunn threw his head back and laughed heartily. "Oh, he hated those elephants when we were packing them up to head to the docks. This will be such a treat." Doctor Gunn chuckled and kissed the top of his wife's head.

"Who is Raven?" Abbie asked.

"Inspector Raven Clarke. He invited us to come here with him," Laurel said.

"Will he be staying here, too?" Abbie asked, wondering if she had time to settle in another room.

"I believe he was looking for lodgings in town. He was hired as a sort of constable." Laurel said.

"Sheriff." Doctor Gunn corrected.

"I heard the free miners were looking to hire a private detective. They believe the constable is in the pocket of the Alchemists," Abbie said.

"I will mention Raven to your father and if he hasn't already made arrangements, we'll see to it," Laurel assured her.

"Very good. I'll see you at breakfast then?" Abbie asked.

"Certainly," Laurel and her husband answered in unison.

Abbie couldn't help but smile as she shut the door. As she'd watched Laurel and her husband, their closeness caused tightness in Abbie's chest. She was sure she'd never had a relationship with the opposite sex where they stood on equal footing. Sam Brownsmith taught her men didn't respect women who worked in their realm. Men seemed to question everything, whether they were smart enough, talented enough, or could swing a hammer. Granted, mining was hard work and most of the miners were men, but to resign the women of Archangel to a few small careers – if one could call time spent on their back a career – was stupidity personified.

Putting on her coat Abbie shrugged off her anger. She headed out to her coach steam-powered by a pair of brass horses who creaked and stomped as if ready to get underway. She grabbed her cage of avian samples and donned her father's old Busby and made her way to the coach.

Once inside, she punched in the coordinates on the panel in the front of the coach and the horses took off at a trot. It was the optimum setting. You could set the coach to gallop, but it required more coal in the beasts. She didn't have time to use the walk setting, as she may already be late.

She looked forward to sharing the new samples. The doctor she was meeting with did some wonderful work with men who had been injured in the Alchemist run mines and laboratories.

Abigail gathered up some of the iridescent colored canaries which changed color to camouflage into the background. They were nearly invisible. The doctor was looking for a less intrusive way to monitor her patients. Abigail had trained the canaries to sense problems and change color to indicate an emergency. She and Trumbo worked with the Canaries on how to detect distress in patients by interruptions in breathing, increased heartbeats, and even skin discoloration. On display was an ideal home for her canaries that were not quite suited to the mines.

Her carriage came to a slow smooth stop and she stepped out, walking to the boarded sidewalk, and knocked on the door at the end of the long street.

The door opened, and she was greeted. "Abigail, I'm glad you could make it, come on in."

Abbie took in the white apron with some spots of blood and said, "I can come back later Doctor Pembrooke."

"Nonsense. I've finished with my patient. I insist you come in." Doctor Sophia Pembrooke stood aside, granting Abigail entrance into her small office.

*I*nspector Raven Clarke watched as two brass horses trotted down the driveway, he'd almost been run over by the beasts. There was no driver to curse or shout at. He wondered if anyone was even in the coach.

It wasn't the first set of brass animals he'd seen here, and certainly not the most unusual.

He'd finally reached the door and rapped it harder than necessary. A short balding man answered. He was rather unkempt with his starched shirt nearly swallowing his neck and his bowtie crooked and frayed from misuse. "Yep," was all he said.

"Inspector Raven Clarke, I believe Doctor and Mrs. Gunn are staying here, I'm expected for dinner," Raven said.

"The Copper?"

"Inspector," Raven clarified.

"Same thing, they're in the dining room." The little man grumbled and ran his finger under his collar before pointing down the hall.

Raven made his way through a large passage, his boots clicking against the dark stone floor. The passageway had a large mural full of animals in various habitats. The painting was so lifelike that Raven reached out and touched the bison placed on a prairie. The velvety texture beneath his fingers felt so real. He wondered how the painter had accomplished the facade. The large beast made him homesick, but he had important work here. Seward wanted more information and Washington's politicians were still trying to smooth over England's Queen, who was none too pleased with Laurel Gunn's defection to Russian territory.

He reached the dining room to find a white-haired gentleman at the head of the table. Laurel and Ben were seated on his right and Moody on his left. Their mouths falling silent at this sudden appearance.

"My apologies, I was sent in this direction." Raven stumbled over the words. It wasn't his fault the inept butler hadn't shown him back.

"It's alright, Raven, Professor Phelan doesn't stand on ceremony. Have a seat." Laurel directed him to the chair next to Moody.

"Moody," Raven nodded at the boy.

"Inspector," Moody flashed him a toothy smile.

"Scamp," Raven muttered under his breath and ruffled Moody's dark hair before taking his chair.

"Laurel tells me you are taking the private inspector position with the free miners," Professor Phelan asked.

"Yes." Raven laid the napkin on his lap, evaluating the man's manner and appearance.

"Good, good." Professor Phelan said. "Did you find a place to stay?"

"I've decided to stay in Igloo City," Raven answered

"You could stay here if you want?" Laurel offered.

Raven looked to Professor Phelan for confirmation.

"It is fine, I don't mind. I never intended this house to remain empty for this long," the professor answered.

"Did you expect to remarry?" Laurel asked.

"God no! I expected Abigail to be married by now. I was hoping to hear the pitter, the patter of little feet, something besides Trumbo," Professor Phelan said.

"Where is Trumbo?" asked Doctor Gunn, or 'Doc' as Raven preferred to call him. The humor in his voice was unmistakable, as he looked at Raven from across the table.

"I left him in the kitchen, he is a fascinating creature," Moody said.

"That is too bad," said Doc.

Raven looked at Doc. What did he mean?

"Were you expecting Abigail to come home?" Laurel asked.

"Hard to say? Usually, when she goes into town, she comes back late. Honestly, we wouldn't be having dinner if you weren't staying here." Professor Phelan added.

"I'm sorry to put you out," Laurel commented.

"No, bother. Glad to have the company. What's on your mind child? You might as well get on with it."

"I'm not sure if you know the circumstances of my birth…" Laurel paused. She looked down and smoothed her skirt fabric beneath her hands.

Doc stilled her hands beneath the table.

Professor Phelan nodded sympathetically, "Wondering if I knew you were half-fae?"

Laurel's head shot up. "Yes."

"After your mother died, I suspected you might be. May I ask what kind?"

"I recently discovered I'm a half banshee."

Professor Phelan paused for a moment. He set down his fork and took in each person at the table. "There's not a human among you is there?"

"No," Doc replied. "Is that a problem?"

"Not at all." The professor waved his hand dismissively. "Are you all banshees?"

"I'm afraid not," Raven interjected.

"What then?"

"Doc is a gargoyle. Moody is a djinn and I'm a werewolf."

"Wolf or werewolf?" Professor Phelan asked.

"What's the difference?" Moody asked.

"Most of the natives around here possess inner spirit animals. And when the animal takes over they shift fully into animal form. Like a polar bear, or killer whale. So, when your animal takes over do you become a wolf?" The professor gave Raven a hard stare.

"No," Raven muttered. How dare this old man preach on matters he didn't understand?

"So, werewolf, you are stricken with lycanthrope disease."

"I don't understand. Can you clarify?" Moody asked.

Raven harrumphed.

"Most of the wolves in Europe are gone, if not extinct. Lycanthropy moved through during the Middle Ages. It was a disease that affected the wolves to the extent they couldn't fully transition. Some believe witches in league with the Fae created a cursed potion and poisoned castle water supplies. Others believe it is a side effect of the bubonic plague and still others think wolf lines have been diluted from breeding with humans."

"How do you know this?" Moody asked

"We have an entire library full of books including a section on mythology."

"Are you human?" Raven asked in a tense clipped voice.

"Very much so. I don't have any royal blood that I'm aware of, and Abbie doesn't seem to be anything other than human." Professor Phelan wiped his hands on his napkin and rang a small bell on the table.

"Does Abbie know about such things?" Moody asked. The boy was always full of questions.

"She's read all the mythology, but I'm not sure if she truly believes it. She has yet to see someone transform. Though supernaturalism stands before her every day, unless they transformed before her eyes, she would choose not to believe. She relies more on science."

"Nothing wrong with science," Doc said.

"Do you think we should keep such things from her?" Laurel asked.

"I'll leave that in your capable hands, had her mother lived, perhaps she would have believed."

"Why is that?"

"Abbie's mother was a witch, descended from the Salem witches, in fact," Professor Phelan answered.

"I had no idea," Laurel said.

"No, you wouldn't. We kept it a secret, and as my wife was a solitary practitioner, there was no reason to bring Abbie into the practice when I didn't understand it. Magick was one of the things that your father and I bonded over, given your mother's background. If your mother had lived, perhaps Abbie would've been a believer."

"Perhaps." Laurel smoothed her hands over her skirts. Raven recognized the gesture as something she did whenever she became uncomfortable.

Before dessert could be brought out, Raven's nose caught a whiff of blood on the wind as cool air from outside came rushing down the hall to the dining room.

Ben and Moody turned their heads as well, and Laurel began that slow keening foreboding of death.

The small butler moved urgently into the room shouting, "Mr. Phelan, Miss Abigail is back and covered in blood, something is wrong with her sir!"

The Professor rose and charged down the hallway to the front parlor.

They were greeted with utter chaos. In the front parlor stood a blond girl wavering on her feet. Her blue irises stark against the white of her eyes and so much blood. It was as if she showered in it. A man rotund and surprisingly short gripped her arm like a vice.

"Professor Phelan, we'll be charging Miss Abigail with the murder of a Free Miner." The man thrust Abigail forward and she stumbled, her boots sliding on the now wet, black and white tiled floor.

Ben caught her, setting her at arm's length, he looked at Raven and gave him a stare before asking the Professor. "Where can Laurel and I take Abbie to get her cleaned up?"

"Take her to her lab down by the conservatory, you should have everything you need there," Professor Phelan answered.

"Where did you find the girl?" Raven asked.

"This is official business, sir. I'm not answerable to you." The man puffed up like a peacock in his royal blue suit.

"Constable Belle, let me introduce Inspector Raven Clarke. He's been hired by the Free Miners to investigate things like murder."

"My apologies, sir. Constable Vernon Belle, I'll be happy to help with your investigation, but Abigail Phelan was found over the deceased."

"Why didn't you arrest her straight away?" Raven asked.

"Oh, I wanted to, but Cameron Jones was having none of it. He wanted her brought home straight away."

"Cameron Jones is the leader of the Free Miners," Professor Phelan supplied.

"Let us head off to the scene." Raven grabbed his coat from the butler, who stood at the ready.

"I've already looked at the scene. The body is no longer there." The Constable balked.

"Well I'd like the body moved to my office in town, and Moody and I'll review the scene. Moody!"

The boy stepped silently forward as if he'd been waiting to be summoned. "Inspector?"

"Gather your coat and notebook, we have our first crime."

CHAPTER THREE

"$\mathcal{A}$bbie, Abbie! Can you hear me?" Laurel waved her hands in front of Abbie.

Abbie heard her. She just couldn't vocalize what had happened. Her voice was trapped like a copper vein in the deepest shaft.

"My heart, I think she's in shock."

Abbie turned her head towards the male voice.

"I know, Ben. I want her to snap out of it."

"She's looking right at me. Aren't you, my girl?" Doctor Gunn asked.

Abbie nodded, her voice dead.

"You don't have to talk to Miss Phelan." Doctor Gunn said. "Mrs. Gunn and I are collecting some samples. Laurel will get you cleaned up. Does that sound reasonable?"

Abbie blinked, mute. She realized she'd been brought to her lab for testing. She pointed over Doctor Gunn's shoulder to steel cabinets in the corner of the room

"Over here." Even as he spoke, he'd begun moving towards the cabinets. His hands slid over the top and gathered her first aid box, as well as some tweezers, vials, and other items.

He set the items on a cart she usually wheeled around the conservatory, but it was fine, as everything in her lab was sterile beyond reproach.

"Alright, Laurel, you want to begin wiping her face with these towels and I'll start gathering samples." Doctor Gunn worked meticulously gathering tiny hairs from her with a pair of tweezers, dropping some dried blood in vials, and cutting swatches off her clothing.

Abbie didn't mind, she would never wear the dress again.

"Do you recall what happened?" Laurel searched her eyes as if to probe into her thoughts.

She opened her mouth, but no sound came out, her voice froze if she tried to articulate anything. She shook her head and a tear slipped from her eye.

Abbie couldn't recall anything before arriving in the parlor of her home. She looked down. What happened? She went to town to meet with...someone. Her mind was fuzzy. She remembered leaving the house but beyond that moment the memory disappeared like mist on a bog penetrated by the sun. She shuddered.

"I'm sorry." Abbie's voice broke through the hushed stillness.

"It's okay, Ben and I will figure out what happened. You are safe." Laurel encircled Abbie in her arms, squeezing her.

"If I think beyond leaving the house to meet with--" She threw Laurel's arms off her and bent over protecting her head in her trembling hands.

"Are you in pain?" Doctor Gunn asked.

She nodded. "Only when I try to remember."

"Don't force it then, just rest." Laurel rubbed her back. "We will find the answers."

Abbie nodded and refused to believe she'd done something horrible, despite the evidence gathered which was damning.

True to their word, once Doctor Gunn finished collecting samples, Laurel readied a bath. The house baths were just off the conservatory and utilized the hot springs prevalent in Alchemia.

"I'm truly envious of this personal bathing room you have." Laurel collected the discarded clothing.

Abbie nodded her agreement and sank herself into the tub. As with all things, the water heated by the springs healed all aches and pains. Her memory loss was no exception. She ached as if she'd been scratching at ore all day with a pickaxe.

"Would you like some laudanum? I believe Ben has some in his bag."

"No. I'll be fine. My apologies for dampening your arrival." She was ashamed at creating such a scene and others believed the worst.

"Nonsense. I've had my fair share of drama. Don't worry, we'll sort all this out." Laurel reassured her.

There was knocking on the other side of the door. Through the cedar, Abbie could hear the muffled sounds of Trumbo as if he was pouting on the other side.

"Can you let him in?" she asked Laurel.

Laurel stood and opened the door.

"Thanks, he would've made such a racket until he got his way." Abbie watched as her brass pet lumbered into the room.

Trumbo sensed there was something awry with his mistress. He padded over to the tub, his feet clinking on the natural stone mosaic tiles. Once he reached the edge, he dipped his trunk in the water and blew warm bubbles.

Abbie laughed.

Laurel paused at the door and spoke quietly with a smile, "I'll let you two have a moment."

"Thank you for your help."

"Of course," she spoke over her shoulder just before the door closed with a click.

"Trumbo, whatever am I going to do?"

He lifted his trunk and tilted his head as if pondering her question.

"I wish I could remember." Abbie swallowed the despair in her throat and sank deeper into the water.

* * *

RAVEN STARED down at the corpse. It was a gruesome sight and he doubted Professor Phelan's daughter was capable of such strength. The victim was missing an arm and there were slashes to his chest, serrated yet imprecise like a beast.

"Looks like the Cleaver," Moody said.

"Yet, we know it's not." Raven was uncomfortable, knowing that particular foe lay in hell.

Moody merely nodded in agreement and penciled in his notebook.

"Gentleman," Constable Bell interrupted. "This is Mr. Cameron Jones, he insisted Miss Abbie be returned home and this miner is his.

"He's not mine. He is employed with the Free Miners. There is a difference Belle," Mr. Jones ripped the words out with disapproval.

Cameron Jones stood at nearly six feet. Age lowered his stature. His dark graying hair stark against his fragrant black bear coat. He wore a dark leather hat with a brim wide enough to shield his features.

Raven rose and shook the man's hand in greeting. "Sorry to meet you under these circumstances, sir."

"And he is?" Mr. Jones lifted his face to Moody. Large claw-like scars ran from right to left down the man's face, partially hidden by a gray beard that was rubbed to a point. While his left eye held a steely gaze on Moody, the right one was a milky whitish gray, and damaged from an attack by what Raven guessed to be a bear.

"Moody Jinn, sir," Moody responded. "I'll be assisting Inspector Raven." Moody went back to scribbling in his notebook.

"Fine, fine." Mr. Jones thrust his hands in his pockets and asked, "You're the new Inspector my boy, Malcolm, hired?"

"He and a few others," Raven agreed. "So, who is our victim?"

"This is the night foreman, Cornelius Turner."

"Tell me what you know about Mr. Turner."

"He started as a canary courier about five years ago and worked his way up." Mr. Jones said his expression grave and his voice devoid of any emotion.

"Canary courier?" Moody asked.

"Our canaries are supplied by Abigail Phelan. It's a nice entry-level position for young'uns getting into mining. Personally, I think Edmund just wanted his daughter to meet eligible young men." Mr. Jones said with a chuckle.

"You'd think there'd be a better way to keep a man safe in the mines," Raven said off-handedly.

"What do you mean?" asked Moody, a pencil held at the ready.

"Letting the canaries die from the fumes."

Cameron Jones threw back his head with a laugh.

"What is so humorous, sir?" Raven wondered if the man was sane.

"Have you toured Miss Abigail's aviaries, Inspector?" asked Jones with a smile which accented the weather-beaten lines of his face.

"No." Raven shifted uncomfortably, sensing he was the butt of a joke.

"Abigail breeds her canaries to change color based on different toxic fumes. Rest assured no canaries are harmed."

Raven looked to Moody, who merely nodded in agreement.

"You could've spoken up Scamp," Raven chastised him.

"And miss this moment, I think not." Moody looked back to the corpse and began writing on his pad.

"Back to Mr. Turner," Raven growled.

"Yes. As I said Cornelius was our night foreman and he'd been doing a good job."

"Any enemies?" Moody asked.

"Not near as I know. He was fair to all the men, and I'd never heard even one complaint."

"Possible bear attack?" Raven suggested.

"Not a bear," Jones said stoically.

"The scratches across his chest are consistent in size and a grizzly can rip a man's arm off."

"I know bears, Inspector, and this was no bear." Jones insisted.

Raven wondered why the man didn't wear a patch. Raven's own eye was missing from bayonet damage, and he covered his ghastly wound with a patch more to comfort others than protect his vanity. Perhaps Cameron Jones meant to unsettle.

"We don't have much of a bear population." Constable Belle said to no one in particular.

Jones harrumphed, clearly not in agreement.

"Do you have any other animals that could remove a man's arm and if not a beast, why take a man's arm?"

"That's easy, it's an automaton," Constable Belle stated as if the motive was obvious.

"What?" Raven and Moody spoke quickly. It was hard to decide who asked first.

"It's not real. He could've been killed for his arm. We've had this sort of thing happen at the Alchemist mines. Once the miner is removed it is sold part by part or whole on the Scavenge Market." Constable Belle puffed up as he bragged about his knowledge.

"Scavenge Market?" Raven was curious.

"The market is further inland, closer to the Yukon Territory, so the pirates can clear out when the Russians raid them." Cameron Jones supplied additional information when Vernon Belle became tight-lipped. "I admit if there are Scavengers in the Free Mines, I want to put a stop to it."

"How long has Cornelius had his mechanical arm?"

"For as long as I've known him," Jones said in a clipped tone.

"How long have the Scavengers been in the area?"

Constable Belle spoke up, "They've been particularly devious the past few months."

"Oh?" Raven was intrigued.

"Yes, and before Cornelius worked for the Free Miners, he worked for the Alchemist Mining Syndicate. It's possible the arm was placed by them, in which case it's forfeited to them upon Mr. Turner's death." Vernon Belle strutted about, seemingly back in his element of informing others of the importance of his involvement.

"And Miss Abigail had the arm in her possession when you apprehended her?" Moody asked, knowing the answer.

Raven would have to commend the boy on his ingenuity.

"No!" Cameron Jones replied vehemently. "And that's exactly why I had Vernon take her home straight away. There is no possible way Abigail did this." Cameron waved his hand at the carnage.

"See here Mr. Jones. I had every right to take Miss Phelan into custody. She remains the prime suspect."

"Why? Because she stood dumbfounded over the deceased?" Cameron shook his head and fisted his hands at his sides.

"She was covered in the victim's blood," answered Constable Belle.

"Gentleman, please. Mr. Jones, this is why your son hired me to investigate crimes about the Free Miners. Constable Belle, if you wouldn't mind checking on the ownership of the victim's mechanical appendage that would be helpful. If it turns out to be the property of the Alchemist Mining Syndicate, we will work the case together."

"At least someone can be reasonable," Belle huffed. He stormed off, in the direction of the Alchemist Mining Syndicate.

"You know he'll drum up evidence to involve himself in the investigation," Jones said.

"I suspected as much. Why do you believe he will?" Raven asked.

"The same reason he tried to arrest Abigail. His money, position, and power come from the Syndicate. They would like nothing more than to ruin Edmund."

"Wouldn't they rather ruin you, sir?" Moody asked.

"Hell yes, but if they ruin me, the next in line takes over, and so forth, and so forth. The Syndicate would have to kill every Free Miner to take over the free mines. If they ruin Edmund then it would force us to buy mining supplies from the Syndicate on their script. The Phelan's take everything on trade or direct purchase."

"How are you able to get supplies?"

"Smuggling." Jones smiled.

"What?" Raven couldn't believe he'd been in the house of a smuggler.

"Don't look offended, Inspector. Edmund still has ties to the English government as well as allies in America. He's the only one that can get supplies through Russian customs controlled by the Syndicate." Jones explained.

"I see." It didn't sound nefarious, but Raven was still uncomfortable with it.

"Abigail didn't kill Cornelius. I would suspect the Syndicate had a hand in it, but Vernon brings up legitimate concerns regarding the Scavenge Market."

"Perhaps we should investigate the market?" Moody's eyes gleamed and Raven sensed his enthusiasm.

"Come by the office tomorrow and I'll have Malcolm get your directions."

"Do you know anything about the market, Mr. Jones?" Raven was willing to travel, although he doubted it would be promising. He did need to know where the criminal element did business.

"I don't, but I have contacts that do," he said, lowering his head.

"Alright, I'd like to have Mr. Turner examined."

"The only doctor in town works for the Syndicate. She would probably be able to give you a preliminary?"

"No need. I have a physician. Can you have Mr. Turner brought to my office?"

"Certainly. Are you the physician?" Jones nodded at Moody.

"No, that would be my father, Doctor Gunn," he replied.

"The building next to yours used to be a doctor's office. I'm sure the miners would be happy to have a doctor again if your friend is interested."

"Why is it vacant?" Raven asked.

"The Syndicate built new offices right off their mine, abandoning the older buildings. Your office used to belong to Belle, so you even have a jail cell," Jones explained.

"I'll talk to Doctor Gunn. I'm sure he'd love to help."

"I'll have Cornelius brought there, and I'll see you tomorrow, Inspector." Cameron Jones said in parting.

"Until tomorrow." Raven turned to leave hearing Moody behind him.

"What do you think of Cameron Jones?" Moody asked.

"Well at his age, he's a wealth of information and a well of secrets wrapped into one man. I guarantee Mr. Jones knows more than he's telling us."

"Is he a suspect?"

"I think Cameron Jones is capable of many things. It seems unlikely that a man like him would kill Mr. Turner for his arm. He didn't smell like blood, and he's fully capable of concealing a crime of this magnitude, rather than calling in the law and risking the Phelan girl's involvement."

"It draws suspicion away from him, though," insisted Moody.

"No. He has a general fondness for your hosts. I don't believe he would risk their involvement. You've met Abigail Phelan, is she capable of the crime."

"I don't believe so. She's smart and the scene looks primal as if without thought, like you said, a beast."

"She's descended from a witch; perhaps she created a formula that made her strong?"

"Maybe. I can investigate her research, while I'm staying at the house."

Raven nodded in agreement. "I didn't realize Alchemia was full of Fae. You may want to consider Fae who are powerful and beastly."

"Like a werewolf." Moody cuffed him on the shoulder.

"Just so."

CHAPTER FOUR

Raven ordered Mister Turner's body placed in the doctor's office, adjacent to his own. There were living quarters in his office in the back and he opted to stay there, rather than at Igloo City. It was in town and close to the mines, should incidents arise or people needed help.

The day after Cornelius Turner was found; Doc looked the corpse over and commented. "Boy, quite a beastie must've done this. Look at tears through the muscle." He held his spying glass up to examine the rips more closely.

"I'm good." Raven stood in the doorway. "Constable Belle believes it was a bear."

"I thought the Constable believed Abbie to be the culprit."

Raven raised his brows. "Do you think her capable?"

"No. She's a bit of a thing. Shorter than Laurel. In looking at these tears, though, I have a hard time believing even a bear is capable of such a thing."

"Much experience with bears?" Raven asked.

"We had them in the circus, although now I have to wonder if they were perhaps shifters. It's funny to have your world turned upside down."

Unlike Raven, Doc was unaware of his status as Fae until last year when he rekindled his romance with Laurel. He'd believed he was human. What a luxury that must've been. Raven always knew he was different, first part savage, and later wolf – not purebred though. He didn't know about the Lycanthrope gene, although it explained his inability to fully shift. His Chippewa cousins had said it was because he wasn't pure. He was polluted by his father's blood. In a way it was true, his father's family had survived the disease which ravaged the wolves of Europe and now he bore the defect of his ancestors' survival. Raven shook off his thought's trying to listen to Doc's voice.

"...not serrated like a blade, but cleaner than an animal. I would suspect a large bear to leave scratches and other indicators, hair, saliva, blood possibly, but this body is clean, relatively speaking. The only blood on here is Mr. Turner's."

"Are you certain?"

"I'll type it and confirm with the microscope, but I doubt I will find anything. Was there a significant amount of blood at the scene?" Doc asked.

"Pooled around his torn arm, but there was no trail if that's what you're wondering."

"Did it spray in a pattern from his arm, or was there just a puddle?" Doc asked.

"A puddle." Raven wondered when Doc got so morbid.

"That means his heart wasn't pumping when he died. And yes, I know something about hearts." Doc's humor came through recalling he'd had a clockwork heart for some time.

"Well, that leads me to the motive of his being killed to sell his automaton arm. What's the cause of death then?"

"I suspect he ingested poison. I've not found any knife, bullet, or another type of injury. No visible needle marks, but I should have an answer after I've completed my autopsy. Should have it for you the morning after the ball."

"Okay, well I'll interview Miss Phelan, then." Raven turned ready to leave.

"I wouldn't," Doc said.

"Why ever not? Look Doc, I know she's Laurel's friend, but I've got an investigation to run." Raven wondered if perhaps the Gunn's were too close to this case since Laurel's childhood friend was involved.

"She doesn't recall the events. And when she tries, she suffers from terrible headaches. Her condition is as if her mind wants her to forget."

"How do you propose I prove her innocence, if I can't get her side of the story?"

"After the ball, you'll have my report and you can get her story. I'm hoping it's some sort of shock amnesia and she's forcing the memories, so they aren't coming. Just give her a few days."

So Raven did.

Two days passed without incident leading up to the day of Laurel's homecoming ball. During the time Raven resettled in his office flat. He found a door in the hallway between the buildings leading to the physician's office while moving the sparse furniture items. He didn't feel the need to tell Doc about it just yet.

The house connecting via the hallway to the sheriff's building belonged to a couple of whores, before the new laws had gone into effect. Raven supposed the design was for efficiency, either personal or professional, both the law and the doctor had set up shop here. As the house was attached and abandoned, he was able to claim the property. All the furniture, but the beds were still in the house. So he moved his bedroll into one of the lower bedrooms and had stayed in the room with the faded foam green wallpaper the last couple of nights.

The jail was still intact if he needed it, and there was more than enough room in the house, too much for just him. Perhaps he'd invite Moody to stay with him. He'd only need one bedroom, and he thought perhaps Doc could use some of the others for patients. Yes, this should work out just fine.

* * *

Despite the revelry of Laurel's homecoming, the ball darkened his mood. He recalled attending a few events after the war, but he'd always understood he was out of place, as his brethren were not welcome in the host's homes, due to their savage looks. Bearing more the appearance of his father, he passed for English, with his odd accent, a mix of the Queen's English, and his mother's native tongue. People couldn't quite place it. Once he revealed he was American, it was accepted.

Raven hadn't spoken with Phelan's daughter yet; as he found it unlikely she could do any real harm. He had yet to see the chit, however. Given the trauma of the scene, he was willing to wait, and allow her time to lay distance between the murder and her emotions. He admitted to not liking the emotional interview to come.

He headed to the bar to get a drink and halted upon hearing the next names called.

"Lady Laurel Gunn presented with her husband Doctor Benjamin Gunn!" The butler George called out in the clearest Raven had ever heard him speak. His livery was even on straight, it was as if he'd been ironed along with his clothes.

Raven watched the door for Phelan's daughter. He'd assumed she would be announced towards the end of the procession as women entered wearing jeweled dresses with matching birds on the hats. The unnecessary need for bird feathers as a fashion accessory had nearly caused the extinction of the cardinal, bluebird, and other brilliant birds.

He turned away, refusing to gape at the audacious display. He wished he was anywhere but here.

The women moved away from their partners, except Laurel who stood with her head close to her husband. The ladies began lining along the white cobbled walkway and each removed her hat, raising it to form a bridge.

"What utter nonsense," he muttered.

A patron next to him chuckled. "This is the best part," he said.

Raven watched as the music played again with a thoughtful flute sound. The birds on the hats began to change color and wriggle on the brims. Violins were added to the flute and the birds stretched their wings out as if to prepare for flight.

Raven stood dumbfounded. There had been no indication the birds were alive. He couldn't comprehend what to make of this living performance before him. He'd never seen anything like it.

He stepped forward to try and catch the view as more people crowded to watch the spectacle.

The birds flapped and stood before taking flight. Initially, they fluttered to the top of the room and formed into a rainbow of color before diving back towards the women and again up to the ceiling and back down towards some men enjoying their port. They flew from the gentlemen over towards the bar where Raven stood. The blasted birds were headed right for him.

He ducked as he heard the bartender laugh.

The birds had risen towards the chandelier and swirled like a tornado of color.

He watched as small groups of them broke formation to head towards the conservatory tunnel on the other end of the room.

Raven stared across the room at the girl who was shuffling birds a large row of cages on wheels. She was hardly noticeable, so ordinary. She wore dun-colored overalls similar to those worn by aeromechanics. The shapeless suit did not indicate the type of figure beneath. Her blond hair hung in two braids nearly to her waist.

He watched her.

She shuffled birds like a hawker shuffling cups. She grabbed them out of the air and sorted them proper.

Red in one cage

Blue in another.

Orange in the very last one on the right.

She turned. Her skin was like the Luna moon, with a dusty path of freckles across her nose and cheeks. Her eyes were the color of the dancing sea. Blue and bright you could get lost in the depths.

"I see you've met our Miss Phelan," a voice behind him broke his siren's spell.

"That's Abigail Phelan?" He turned to see his informant.

The woman before him was the very image of Molly Flannigan. The only differences were storm gray eyes and black hair.

"Molly?" he had to know.

"No. I'm Emma, Emma Flannigan." She eyed him with suspicion. "How do you know my sister?"

"I knew your sister in Constantinople."

"Oh? And how is Molly?"

"I'm sorry, your sister she's no longer --"

"Excuse me." Emma lifted her skirts and fled as if Raven himself had killed Molly.

Raven turned back to where Abigail Phelan had been standing to find she was no longer there without a sign of her either. The birds were all in their cages, eating, drinking, and making their own music.

Raven navigated his way through the bustle of skirts, and men leaning on canes to find Laurel and Doc.

* * *

ABIGAIL SHOOK off the stare of the amber eye stranger with the patch.

She'd hidden behind the birdcages when he'd spoken with Emma. When she saw Emma flee as if the devil were behind, she decided it best to remain hidden.

She watched as he moved between the patrons as a wolf weaves between trees, nearly a direct line unless there is an obstruction. A lady with a wine glass nearly spilled it but he seemed to narrowly miss getting hit.

"I thought I'd find you here."

Abigail turned away from the mysterious man.

Malcolm Jones stood before her. He was a handsome man, a few years older than her with dark brown hair and ice-blue eyes. He was tall and she had to crane her neck simply to speak to him. His person was always meticulously neat, to the point where she wondered how he managed. When he was at the office, he was always working with ink and surrounded by the elements of the mine. It was an impossible task to keep clean, but even as she looked at his fingers, the nails were spotless of his profession.

"I'm surprised to see you here. You usually refrain from attending such events, wishing to catch up on your beauty rest." Abigail teased him, the Camerons were known for not attending late events in the fall and winter. They were known as heavy sleepers.

"You are correct, but I need to meet with someone." He covered his mouth with his well-manicured fingers to hide his yawn.

"Did your father come too?" She looked beyond Malcolm hoping to catch a glimpse of the cantankerous Cameron.

"No. He is resting up. He needs his rest more now that he's older," Malcolm said.

"Oh," Abigail said, unable to disguise her disappointment. "Who are you here to see?"

"I think the man you were spying on." Malcolm smiled. He had caught her surveillance.

"I'm simply curious. A girl can't be too cautious with unfamiliar men.

"True."

"Who is he? Do you know?"

"Inspector Raven Clarke. We hired him privately. He is investigating the death of Cornelius."

Abigail swallowed. The mere mention of the poor miner gave her a headache. She simply couldn't form an image of the night's events. She'd been told Constable Belle considered her the main suspect. Disorientation and disbelief warred with the reason she could harm anyone, especially Cornelius who helped her with her canaries.

He would always keep the new handlers in line, letting them know she wasn't for them and the young men best toe the line or feel his wrath. She couldn't imagine a man who took the time to tell the difference between canaries and name them as having a temper, let alone wrath.

Did something happen and she was forced to defend herself and kill? The thought made her nauseous.

"Are you going to have me arrested?" She asked, unable to quell the panic in her voice. She knew Cameron Jones had prevented the Constable from having her hauled away in irons, but no one had spoken to her since Cornelius's murder.

"Abbie, of course not." He reached his hand toward her.

"Then why are you meeting with the Inspector?"

"To see what he has uncovered." He tilted his head to the side and said, "I'm surprised you haven't been interviewed by him."

"I've been busy, but I would've made the time to help." She shuffled her feet from side to side.

"Well, why don't you come with me and we can see what he's uncovered." He began walking toward the Inspector who stood with Laurel and her husband.

"Yes, I think I will." She shook off any embarrassment at her state of dress. She knew Laurel wouldn't care and who gave a hoot what the handsome Inspector thought. She was trying to prove her innocence, not snare a suitor.

"'Scuse me, Abbie," George spoke behind her.

"Yes, George," she sighed. She knew what was coming.

"Your father wishes to speak at you. Sorry," he nodded an apology at Malcolm.

"Understood." He gave Abbie a light squeeze on her shoulder.

"Malcolm, I--"

"Abbie, it's not good to avoid a confrontation with one's parent, trust me." He turned to walk away. Malcolm had dismissed her.

"Alright, George. Lead the way." Abbie shoved her hands in her pockets, and shuffled after George, preparing her argument for Papa's lecture.

* * *

Sophia Pembrooke hung back watching events unfold in Phelan's Conservatory. She was almost relieved that she'd accepted Boris Baranov's invitation. Her berating thoughts subsided as he fell deeper into his cups.

Boris hadn't wanted to leave his game of cards to watch the parade of birds.

Sophia didn't want to make an appearance given the guests of honor. She already had about as much as she could take of the blasted birds. She'd spent the last week perfecting her formula, to have every bird Abbie gave her killed after Emory had gotten his hands on them. Sophia hadn't expected them to live through the procedure, but to have her husband kill all of them was a disappointment. Worse, she had to somehow procure more, if Abbie had even more of the invisibirds.

She'd watched from a distance when Laurel and Ben were announced. As the Inspector discovered Emma Flannigan, and when Abbie fled to her father's study. Thanks to the automaton hearing aids surrounding her ears, she could hear every word as well.

"Did you know Molly had a sister?" Doctor Gunn asked his wife.

"No, but how much do employers know?" Laurel smoothed her hands on her skirt.

"You were more than her employer, Laurel," Raven accused. "She was one of your closest friends."

Laurel looked to the floor as if the whore could find answers in the tile.

Sophia huffed.

They continued to mutter their surprise Emma was even in Alchemia.

She looked back towards Boris as he continued to drink and lose. He should have more respect for himself and her. The only reason she accepted his invitation was that Boris was supposed to be a pillar of the community. Boris was the head of the syndicate and he'd given her the job of a doctor. He expected results. He wanted to improve the output of the miners by any means necessary. How could he expect to lead people when he was incapable?

She continued to listen while Boris continued toward defeat.

"...Do you think she can see the dead too?"

"She has ghost eyes, so I think so. I wanted to let you know Moody and I will be heading to the Scavenger market in the morning," Raven said.

"I've wanted to go there," Laurel said.

"Whatever for?" The inspector asked.

"To find gargoyles," Doctor Gunn answered.

Unable to resist, Sophia turned her head towards the conversation.

"Gargoyles, whatever would you want with such things?" Malcolm Jones joined their conversation.

"Doctor Gunn and I are thinking of building a castle if we can find land," Laurel remarked.

"Oh?" Malcolm seemed curious.

"My wife misses England and wants a few reminders. Besides, gargoyles guard and bring good luck."

Of course, he would know all about gargoyles, Sophia recalled.

"I'm ready to leave, Soph." Boris grabbed her around the waist.

"My name is Sophia. You may call me Doctor Pembrooke." Sophia untangled herself from Baranov's limbs and took a step back.

"Are you ready to leave this bourgeois place?" Boris sounded suddenly sober compared to minutes ago, which made Sophia question how much liquor he could hold.

"Yes, I've heard enough."

He looked at her puzzled, and she realized her error. "The music is causing the sonics in my ear aides to vibrate."

"Ah. Then let us leave this place." Boris held his arm for her to take and he escorted her away from those who might recognize Sophia from her previous life.

* * *

ABBIE TRAILED her fingers along the bookshelves in her father's study. Books from architecture to the Zulu nation, and everything between. Nothing compared to her books on science and magic here, unless it is related to building something, somewhere. Her father also devoted two walls to the storage of maps. She imagined the maps would be moved into the main library as he continued collecting more and more of them.

The door cringed on its hinges and Abbie turned to see her father enter. He was starting to bend forward with age but still walked reasonably well. He was one of those engineers who liked to be in the thick of it. He was often seen working alongside men on the canals he built as well as in the mines, though he considered himself retired.

"Abigail." He must be upset with her to keep from using his usual 'Poppet'.

"Father." Two could play this game.

He shook his head at her, "Why were you not at the ball?"

"But I was, Papa."

"You know very well what I meant. Did Miss Flannigan not make a gown for you? I know I have a bill somewhere." Her father began rifling through papers on his desk as if somehow the bill of sale would support his right of the argument.

"The ball gown is not yet finished," she said.

"As if an incomplete gown gives you cause to avoid guests and walk around dressed like an aeromechanic." He waved his hand up and down and frowned as if appalled by her appearance.

"And a bill of sale gives you the upper hand?" She asked, curious.

"Of course not. Do not be obtuse." He sat down in the chair behind his desk, apparently exhausted from their battle of wits.

Sensing a change, Abbie sat across from him in her chair. It was the chair she sat in while he worked, occasionally slept, and rarely chastised her, in this office. The leather was particularly worn and the wood faded in spots where she had dangled her legs over the arms as a child. If Abbie leaned forward she'd be able to feel under the desk where she'd carved her name while her father slept one afternoon. Now was not the time. "What's wrong, Papa?"

"I wanted to introduce you to Inspector Raven Clark."

"You did?" Abigail was stunned. What could be the motive behind a formal introduction of one's parent? She hoped this wasn't another lecture on marriage.

"Yes, we need to get in front of Cornelius Turner's brutal murder. I don't think a member of the town believes you are capable of killing."

"I would never." Somehow, the accusation of murder struck her as better than marriage.

"Regardless of what you would or would not do. Most agree you lack the strength demonstrated in the brutality of the deed."

"That's a relief." Abbie wasn't even remotely relieved. The town believed she could kill, just not in a brutal fashion? "If I'm not capable of the crime, why speak with the inspector?'

"Because Baranov wants to use this crime against us. Constable Belle isn't stupid enough to go against his employer."

"Have they asked about purchasing the abandoned mines again?"

"Why buy when they can fabricate a scandal with my daughter and force me to give it to them."

"Is it a scandal?"

"Who bloody knows?" Her father leaned back in his chair. "Belle's latest theory is that you had your jumbo do it."

"Trumbo?"

"Who would've guessed I'd need to have an alibi provided for your pet? Luckily, Mr. Jinn was happy to show Belle through all the tricks he'd taught Trumbo during the time in question. I think Baranov wanted to confiscate him to see exactly what upgrades we'd made to him."

Abbie's breath hitched and she gripped the arms of the chair. The syndicate tried to steal her precious Trumbo. She bit back tears. Trumbo may not be real to others, her father included, but when Sam Brown worked on Trumbo significant upgrades had been made. Her favorite was the clockwork cooling pump which beat like a heart. His high-end sensors allowed him to respond to her feelings, based on her breathing, skin tone, and heartbeat. He was so much more than a machine. She and her father were always at odds with the syndicate, but this made it much more personal. "How can Raven Clarkehelp?"

"He needs your side of the story, Poppet." He leaned forward, resting his elbows on the desk, "You can meet him at breakfast."

"I'll do whatever you need, Papa." Abbie stood and straightened her shoulders. She would keep what was hers. Her father, her land, and her pet. The syndicate could go bother someone else, there was no way they were getting their greedy clutches on anything belonging to her family.

CHAPTER FIVE

$\mathcal{R}$aven sat alone in the Phelan dining room. He arrived early to travel with Laurel and Ben to the Scavenger Market, but the Gunns were still in bed according to the butler, George.

He'd already had one cup of tea and was now working on his poached egg when Abigail Phelan halted mid-step into the room.

Raven stood. "Miss Phelan, I presume?"

"Yes." Her smile was stiff. "Inspector Clarke?"

"Yes." He returned her smile with a warmer one and made a shallow bow. "It would seem we are the only early risers."

She glanced around the room as if someone would materialize and a shade of discomfort crossed her features when she turned back to him. "My father is an early bird, but he's likely eating in his study as is his normal fashion."

He took pity on her discomfort. "Am I sitting in your chair?"

"Not at all. I'm just surprised to find you here." She seated herself opposite him.

"Oh?"

"Since Laurel's arrival, I seem to be one of the last ones out of bed." She smiled at him again. This smile was beautifully natural and warm.

Raven's heart tugged as her lips curved upward. She was more beautiful than he recalled from the night before. Maybe it was her green morning dress which contrasted and complimented her porcelain skin or maybe it was because the sun flashed off her wheat-colored hair.

"How old are you?" He couldn't resist asking.

She shot him a brief glare before concentrating on her plate. "As I suspected, the Gunns have left you alone with me."

"Did they? Whatever for?" Laurel and Ben could not have guessed his attraction to this vulnerable beauty. Could they?

"So you could begin your interrogation of me regarding Cornelius Turner's death." She tilted her head.

He scanned her, evaluating her. "I doubt you had anything to do with Mr. Turner's murder."

She leaned forward, "So foul play is suspected."

"I'm afraid so. What can you tell me about that night?" Raven couldn't help but wonder how this tiny breath of a woman was wrapped up in Alchemia's gruesome murder.

"I can't recollect much from the night of Mr. Turner's murder. I've tried but every time I search my memory, my throat locks up, and I feel my limbs numb and my brain becomes foggy. It sounds strange, I know. Doctor Gunn says my symptoms are similar to shell shock."

"I'm aware of the disorder." His mind burned with the memory of his own experience.

"I'm sorry I can't be of more help. Cornelius was a wonderful man and very kind to me and my birds."

"Tell me about him." Her voice soothed him, despite the fact he found birds as exciting as watching a clock tick.

"Cornelius was my first canary courier. The couriers run the birds to and from the mines. They also have to sit with the fledglings so the birds become used to them. Cornelius even went so far as to watch the hatchlings. He was a surrogate to many of the colored canaries."

"Was he collecting birds from you that night?"

"No. I went to town."

"To meet him?" Raven wondered if more passed between Abigail and Cornelius.

"No to meet with…" Abigail began to rub her temples. "I'm sorry I don't remember."

"It's alright. You do recall going to town."

"No. Wait…Yes! I took a team of brass horses and canaries."

"Brass horses you say." Raven had nearly been run over by a team of brass horses the night he arrived here.

"Yes, but more importantly, I keep an inventory and what I'm doing with my canaries whenever I remove them from my aviary." She leaped from her chair, her skirt scattering her silverware across the table like otters on ice. In her haste, she nearly plowed into George who was bringing her some toast. "Do you know what this means Inspector?" She turned as if his presence just occurred to her.

George stepped back to the doorway.

"What is that, Miss Phelan?"

"I would have a record of whom I gave the canaries to." Abigail Phelan lifted her skirts and proceeded to run down the hall.

Raven followed her rapidly and it was a challenge. She was like a doe running through the forest. Twists and turns down the corridor, past the conservatory which served as a ballroom further down the tunnel. Her green bustle was like the whitetail to him, impossible to hide among all the stones they passed.

When she stopped, he nearly collided with her padded bustle.

She turned with a ledger which he did collide with. "Ouch!"

"You see, right here in line three hundred and fifty-seven, I delivered them to Doctor --" Her voice broke with a start.

"Doctor?"

Abigail's cheeks pinkened. She dropped the ledger and clutched her throat.

"Can you breathe?" he asked.

She shook her head and mouthed 'NO'.

She began to open her mouth like a fish out of water as if somehow she would begin breathing.

He moved to stand behind her.

Her knees buckled and Raven quickly captured her in his arms before she hit the cobbles.

As suddenly as she stopped breathing, he quickly looked to find her chest rise and fall. She was breathing.

Raven lifted his gaze at footsteps approaching

"So they drop at your feet now, Raven?" Laurel looked down at him with hands on hips.

Doc brushed past his wife, to kneel at Abigail's side, "What happened?" He checked her wrist for a pulse.

"I'm not sure." Raven met Doc's accusing green eyes. "I followed her down here because she remembered writing in her ledger on the night of Mr. Turner's murder."

"And?" Doc withdrew a stethoscope out of his bag. He always had his medic bag on hand, as if he expected medical mayhem.

"When she looked at the ledger, she began choking. But once she passed out, she began breathing again. It was the damnedest thing." Raven found the whole incident vaguely disturbing.

"I'm sure. She seems fine now." Doc removed the stethoscope from his ears and placed them back in the bag.

Raven lifted his gaze at the metallic clink on the stone tile. Walking towards them with steam spouting from its trunk and emerald eyes glowing was a jumbo. Raven drew Abigail against him and reached for his Pocket Model Colt ready to kill the beast.

"Stop!" Laurel stood between him and his quarry.

"Move!" Raven motioned with his gun for Laurel to move and gripped Abigail tighter. She was soft and fit snugly against him.

"Holster that thing." Laurel pointed at his gun.

Raven conceded, but only because the creature had stopped advancing. Laurel's strong tone had no impact on his agreement.

Once his gun was holstered, Laurel continued her speech. "This is Trumbo and he is Abigail's pet."

"Pet?" He wondered if Laurel was baiting him.

"Yes, pet. Come now, you must remember the story I told you about the Jumbos and their origin."

Raven had a vague recollection, about a man who made an elephant for his daughter because she had never seen one. So he'd made the brass animal to placate her. "That inventor was Professor Phelan?" Even as he asked, details of the story cleared.

"Trumbo is the prototype that started all the brass creatures. Despite his diminutive size, he's the first. You might say the grandfather of all the steam-powered animals." There was a slight hint of awe in her voice.

The small brass elephant seemed to like her analogy as he flapped his ears and flashed his eyes, mocking Raven, if such behavior was even possible with a machine. "Is it intelligent?"

"Surprisingly so." Doc finally stated his opinion. "He seems to have the proper programming to follow basic commands."

"YOUR MISS-TRESS FAIN-TED," Raven spoke loudly and

enunciated each word while pointing to Abigail. His words seemed to echo off the walls.

"He's not deaf, you numbskull." Laurel exaggeratedly rubbed her ear.

Regardless, the creature marched over to a shelf and scooped his trunk into a jar. He began his clinker-clatter over to his mistress.

Raven watched dumbfounded as the trunk wafted underneath Abigail's nose.

Her cornflower-blue eyes fluttered open. "Okay, okay, Trumbo, that's enough." She waved the trunk away.

"Do you faint often?" Doc pushed his glasses to the bridge of his nose as he held Abbie's wrist for a pulse.

Abigail freed herself from his embrace. He noticed a reddening along the back of her neck.

He missed her warmth against him.

"Hazards when we check the canaries before sending them into the mines. I have my own brand of smelling salts stashed throughout the conservatory in the event I pass out from inhalation." Abigail explained.

Raven helped her stand. "Are you alright?"

"Yes, thank you for catching me." She avoided looking at the book. "We were looking at the ledgers?"

"Do you want to try again?" Raven asked.

She threw her hand up. "No!"

Everyone took a step back except Doc, who inquired, "Why?"

"It sounds crazy, but I feel if I read that name I will pass out again." Abigail took a step towards Trumbo.

Trumbo opened his mouth revealing a tongue hot as an iron poker. He advanced on the ledger like a soldier in battle.

"Are you going to let him destroy the documentation of your work?" Doc asked.

"Trumbo, stop!" Though she gave the order, Abigail looked unsure.

"What if I take the book?" Raven offered, scooped up the book.

"Yes." Abigail's shoulders relaxed. "Take it, and when you are done, rip the last page out and return it."

"What a perfect solution, Abbie." Laurel came and embraced her friend. "Why don't you finish your breakfast? George has kept the meal warm for you and we'll clean up this mess before we head to the Scavenger Market? Trumbo, you go with her."

Abigail waited for Trumbo to match her pace and the two of them headed back to the dining room.

"Well," Laurel said, "Who received the birds that night?"

Raven opened the book and a chill raced down his spine as he read the name scrawled in Abigail's penmanship. "Doctor Sophia Pembrooke."

"Emma, are you listening to me?" Abbie asked. "Are you looking for something?" Since Abbie arrived an hour ago to collect her peacock dress for the ball Emma had been distracted.

"Yes," I'm looking for my spe-...swatch book," Emma answered.

"Why? My dress is all done isn't it?"

"Yes, but I have another customer who wants a riding habit completed right away." Emma closed the golden yellow panel. She wore a full-length patchwork skirt in blues and browns, pieced together with leftover fabric. Emma had on her leather vest corset which laced up the front. Beneath the vest, she wore a white peasant top. Abbie saw the outfit before with a matching leather blazer.

There was no need for extra layers with a corner stove heating the small space.

Abbie removed her black jacket.

The caravan was flamboyant with splashes of fabric draped over the bed, and the assorted threads in tiny dowels on the back of all the chairs, and a sewing machine in one corner which folded in to create a desk were the only signs of her trade. Near the ceiling was a row of cabinets Emma had just peered in, each was outlined in emerald green. The stained glass above depicted gypsies chaining a man to a building. While the dark image disturbed Abbie the glass let a substantial amount of light in.

"I can leave." Abbie rose from the small hope chest she'd sat on.

"No. I'm sorry. I was distracted. Tell me again."

"I couldn't look at the ledger without going into hysterics." Abbie trembled. She shook her head and swallowed hard. Heaviness clung to her. She must find a way to conquer her memory loss from the night of Cornelius Turner's murder. She just had no idea how.

"Hysterics? Abbie, you sound like one of those physicians." Emma practically spat out.

"Actually, Doctor Gunn called it shell shock. It's a term they used in the Army."

"Well I'm not a believer in doctors, but Benjamin Gunn sounds like he might be more intelligent than his counterparts. What did you do with the ledger?"

"Inspector Raven has it. He is going to give it back to me when he's done." She flushed merely mentioning him by name.

"So he believes you innocent?" Emma sat on the chair opposite Abbie, the rainbow of spools hopping as she did so.

"I believe so. And Emma, he's so handsome up close." Abbie knew she was gushing like a schoolgirl yet she couldn't seem to help herself.

"Personally, I thought he had a roguish quality with his patch." Emma grabbed a shortbread cookie and took a tiny nibble.

"Oh, I agree," Abbie admitted she liked the maddening hint of arrogance about him.

"Abigail Phelan, has a young man finally caught your eye?" Emma smiled before taking a sip of tea, which in all likelihood was cold.

"Perhaps, both of them," she giggled.

"Touché." Emma smiled.

"I barely know him, but I feel drawn to him. I can't explain it." Abbie reached for a cookie and bit into the treat, hoping to stop the nonsense coming out of her mouth.

"Lust," Emma said with all the subtlety of a hammer.

Abbie coughed before the cookie choked her. "Emma!"

"Okay fine. Attraction. Your father has sheltered you, perhaps too much." One corner of Emma's mouth was pulled into a modest smile.

"You're not wrong." Abbie didn't bother to disagree with her. She knew her father protected her since her mother's death and more so after they'd left India.

"So where is this Inspector Charming now?" Emma asked.

"He, Moody, and the Gunns went to the Scavenger Market."

"Whatever for?"

"Raven believes Cornelius was killed for his arm, they are going to see if they can find the arm there."

"I'm surprised you didn't go. You love the market."

"To be honest, I was more excited about this dress." Abbie tapped the brown package tied with a twine bow.

"Now you have someone to wear it for."

"The Miner's Melee won't be until the new year. So it could be quite a while before I wear it."

"You are invited to the Crystal Consortium Carnival, aren't you?" Emma asked.

The Carnival was held at the end of November in the town by the Consortium. It was similar to the Melee but it was held in the streets of Alchemia outside the closest open mine. The Carnival arrived in the town to entertain, and the locals sold items for the upcoming holidays and the miners would have a chance to dance, drink and be merry.

"You know Papa and I never attended the event."

"Maybe you should."

"I wouldn't want to get my dress dirty." The ground wasn't always frozen by the time the Carnival was in town. "I can wait until the Melee."

"Alright, I'm just trying to help a girl out. Tell me more about this memory loss you are experiencing."

"Well, whenever I think back on the night of the murder, I freeze up. I tried to tell Raven the name, but I froze completely and as I tried to say the lady's name, my throat closed and I couldn't breathe."

"So it was a lady?"

"Did I say it was? It must've been."

"Maybe I can help."

"I love you Emma, but what can a seamstress do that an Inspector cannot?"

"Abbie, we are once again getting into your sheltered area again." Emma reached across and squeezed Abbie's hand before rising. "I'll see if I can catch your Inspector Charming at the market." Emma donned her leather jacket. "Would you like to join me?" Emma asked as she began stowing items in the caravan.

"I believe I shall." Abbie resolved with a sense of purpose. The drive to solve the mystery of her lost memories was like a baby bird ready to fly - scary, intimidating, but necessary.

* * *

HAWKERS SHOUTED, buyers argued, for the best price, and conversations in tents added to the already deafening noise. Large automaton displays combined with people diving in and out of pathways made Raven dizzy. Smells of food, animals, and human stench assaulted his nose. The Scavenger Market was a bombardment to his senses.

Why had he wanted to come here? He focused on finding any information valuable and worth this suffering.

He forged ahead, through the crowds when his nose caught the scent of her. What was she doing here? They'd left the house hours ago. He'd not been with her long, yet her smell of fresh linen, lavender with a touch of salt tickled his nose. He turned and blazed a new path. His destination keenly in his mind. Find Abigail. The pathways of tents opened into a field of caravans. Providing far more space than their hawker tent counterparts. They also sold wares and were a mix of gypsy caravan & pioneer-style wagons and the occasional buggy box.

An iron giant greeted him, "What is your business here?" He blocked Raven's path.

"Inspector Raven Clark." Raven thrust his arm out to shake hands.

"Vasili O'Toole." Vasili crossed his arms over his chest unimpressed, "State your business," he commanded.

Raven sniffed around before setting his gaze on Abigail.

She was getting down from a caravan pulled by two brass Belgian steeds.

"I'm here to escort Miss Phelan through the market."

Vasili smiled, revealing a row of several gold teeth. "Abigail Phelan?"

"Yes, I'm trying to clear her name of this nasty murder business." Raven shook his head, sensing Vasili had a likeness for Abigail.

"Miss Abbie wouldn't harm a soul. She's got a heart of brass that one," Vasili readily nodded his head.

"May I pass?" he asked.

Vasili turned away from him back to the caravans. "She's just over there with Emma Flannigan," he pointed to where Raven's eye settled.

Vasili's pointing gave Raven just enough room to pass beneath the behemoth's arm.

* * *

ABBIE COULDN'T HELP but stare at Raven. Though she knew the market to be his destination, it was such a large area the odds of them seeing one another seemed so unlikely.

"I didn't expect to run into you," she said.

"Nor I, you." His ink-colored hair fell over his wounded eye. She wondered if perhaps Doctor Sophia could give him a replacement eye.

"Oh!" She doubled over. A sudden sensation as if her skull were being ripped in two. She gripped her head as if trying to piece it back together.

"What is it?" Raven rushed to her and placed a hand on her shoulder.

"Doctor Sophia! She did this?" The memories came flooding back and along with those images pain as if her skull was ripping in two.

"You remember," he gasped and bowed his head close to hers. His voice trailing over her skin in a calming effect.

"Apparently not without a cost." She yanked off her top hat as if the simple action would relieve the pain. It didn't. If anything, the pain was worse. "I don't understand."

"Maybe Ben and Laurel can shed some light on what happened. I'd like to have them look at you again now that your memory has returned."

"That isn't a bad idea." She gripped his arm tightly.

"Do you feel faint?" he asked.

"No... Yes..."

"Here." He lifted her into his arms and began marching through the market.

"Where are we going?"

"I left Ben and Laurel with a gargoyle dealer. They have got to be here somewhere."

"I don't know how you'll find them, this place is a maze, and changes every time I visit."

* * *

UNFORTUNATELY, Miss Phelan was right. Raven couldn't track Doc or Laurel's scent among so many people. His sense of direction, which made him an excellent tracker, was useless among all the machines running in the tents and flying overhead.

He must simply keep her safe. He inhaled searching for fresh air among the sweat, grease, and odors of various foods. He discovered a crossroad, sniffed for clean air, and followed the route. Within minutes they were placed at the perimeter of the bustling market. Through an arch between two tents he found his exit and seconds later they were free.

He looked down and found Abigail staring at him.

"How did you do that?" she asked, staring as if he was both wondrous and eerie.

"I have a knack for tracking."

"What an unusual skill. I'm truly impressed." Her eyes flew upward and she found herself drawn to his strong and daring appeal.

"It's part of my heritage. It came in handy as a soldier, as an investigator in New York, a field agent for Washington, and now an inspector here. "

"I still don't know how you did it. Are you exhausted somehow?" She pushed against his chest indicating she might want to be free.

He continued to hold her.

"Please let me down," she insisted.

At her vocal request, he set her on the ground but held her waist firm until he was certain of her safety. "Are you okay?" he took a deep breath before releasing her.

"Posh," she waved her hand dismissively. "I'm fine."

He wondered if she truly was, or if her brain had suddenly gone in another direction. He noticed similar behavior this morning. As if she needed to quickly process information before it was lost. He wasn't a scientist but wondered if perhaps her mother had cast a spell or if something else unique to Abigail caused her to retain her memory. He recalled she knew nothing of her mother and phrased his next question carefully.

"Miss Phelan, do you know if you possess any special skills or gifts unusual compared to others?"

"Call me Abbie, all my friends do."

"That seems rather informal," Raven admitted he was interested in more than friendship, but he must stay professional until he cleared her name.

"Inspector you just raced through a crowded market with me in your arms, any sense of formality is gone, and likely gossip has already started." Her sense of humor created light in her blue eyes which rivaled a night sky.

He couldn't help but smile. "Miss Abigail perhaps."

"How about we settle on Abigail?"

"Abigail. And you may call me Inspector."

She gave a hoot of a laugh, holding her hands around her middle before rising back up and wiping her eyes. "Oh you are standing on ceremony," she tossed at him.

"Yes, well..." he coughed, suppressing his laughter, "Do you?"

"Do I have a special skill? I'm not sure what you mean. My friend Malcolm Jones is extremely good at numbers. His brain is like an auto-abacus. I seem to have a talent for cross-breeding which is something I've learned through trial and error of many years. I'm not sure that is as much skill as practice." She shook her head as if disappointed in his question.

"What about other talents?"

"Like singing or playing the glass harmonium?"

He shook his head, "I meant more..."

"Paranormal?" She lowered her voice.

"Yes, actually I was under the impression you didn't believe," Raven shook his head and closed his eyes in relief, but it was short-lived.

"One cannot grow up in Alchemia without hearing about shifters, selkies, Baba Yagas and the like. Alchemians are a superstitious lot. Honestly, Inspector, I expected more of you, don't get sucked in by the people's folklore." There was a sharp edge of disenchantment in her voice, which he found distasteful.

"To be honest, I expected you to believe." He told himself there was still a chance for her to find the truth.

"I'm not a little girl. I don't believe in fairies or monsters." Her sea-blue eyes glinted, and she straightened her shoulders, standing taller, yet still, she didn't reach his chin.

"Most people wouldn't believe in birds changing color. They would believe the change to be magical, might even consider what you are doing in your lab, witchcraft," Rave responded.

"Touché, Inspector. I'll grant you leeway that there may be things science can't explain yet." She began walking along the sides of the tents.

"So you find the folklore around you explainable?" he asked, following her.

"Yes."

"And if there isn't an explanation?" How far did her stubbornness run?

"Like any scholar, I propose a hypothesis and then test."

"Does this answer all the unanswerable?"

"No, but the process can become a bit of a hobby." She stopped in her stride to pointedly stare at him. "I suppose much like you investigate crime, I investigate items which I do not understand. I'm surprised you can leave the unanswered resting in unexplained paranormal superstition."

"My mother and her family held many beliefs which settlers did not understand. Supernatural is part of our faith."

"Arguably the unexplained is part of any religion."

"Don't you believe in anything?"

"I believe in man's capacity to do great good and great evil. And I believe fear can create monsters with heroes capable of defeating them. That does not necessarily mean there are such creatures."

"Has anyone told you, Abigail, you are a stubborn woman?"

"My father, every day since I turned sixteen."

Raven caught a smell of smoke reminding him of Moody. "I believe I left Laurel and Ben around here." He grasped her hand and led her between two tents, her skirt pressing against his calves.

Just as they entered the din of voices hollering at one another, Raven nearly collided with Doc. His sudden halt crashed Abigail into him.

"Ooof!" Her soft form pressing into the mass of his hardened body. "Inspector," she grumbled at him while retreating and seeming to collect her person.

"Are you okay?" Laurel asked pointedly, staring at her husband who along with Moody was carrying a large stone gargoyle. "Really, Raven, you could've broken the gargoyle…." Laurel stared past Raven to Abigail "…statue. Abbie, how are you doing?"

"She remembers," Raven spoke quickly. "I was hoping Doc could take a look at her."

"Ben is busy at the moment. Why don't you lend your nose…or tracking abilities to our cause and we can get back to town sooner." Laurel said.

"Certainly. Where are you headed?" Raven asked.

"We are headed to see a man named Vasili O'Toole, who may be able to lend us a cart for our friend here," Moody grumbled from behind the large statue.

"I just met Mr. O'Toole before finding Abigail," Raven said.

Laurel raised an eyebrow inquisitively.

Raven turned back to Abigail to avoid close scrutiny.

"Don't look at me!" Abigail pointed at the Gunns. "I have no idea how you found them, let alone how to find our way back to Emma's caravan," she huffed, before placing her hands on her hips.

"We were told to follow this path out by the hawker," Doc said in a strained voice.

"Let us continue to follow the route then," Laurel advised. "Raven, why don't you take Ben's place and he can bring up the rear with Moody. Abbie, you can walk with me." Laurel held out her hand.

Abigail took it.

Raven didn't blame her. Laurel used her maternal tone to set everyone into line.

They followed Laurel and she would, from time to time, stop and turn her head ever so slightly to get confirmation from Raven as they navigated the market. He was astonished the hawker hadn't led them in circles but the directions remained sound.

Finally, they exited the market to the caravan camp and he saw Vasili O'Toole.

Abigail waved, "Vasili!"

Vasili turned and smiled wide. He wasn't an attractive man. Raven's stomach hardened and he wanted to voice the man's shortcomings.

Laurel turned and glowered at him as if sensing the foreign emotion. "Go ahead Abbie, if you could be so kind as to arrange the cart, I'll wait with the boys." She lingered on the word boys, drawing it out.

Raven watched Abigail's form as she retreated.

"My Heart," Doc called from the back, "We are setting this down while Abbie fetches the cart."

"It's not truly heavy for you is it?" Laurel turned, looking at each man in turn.

"No, but we don't need the locals knowing we possess other than human strength." her husband answered.

"Are you serious? I think half the group here is Fae," she answered.

"More than half," Raven agreed with her. "I didn't smell a single human, but I assume they are just undetectable among the magick as well as the grease and machinery."

Doc whistled. "You weren't kidding when you told us this was a haven."

Moody coughed as Abigail approached with Vasili and a cart.

Laurel looked toward their approaching company, "Not too much trouble was it?"

"Not at all ma'am," Vasili answered. "Any friend of Abbie's is a friend of The Caravan Clan.

"The Caravan Clan?" Moody asked.

"Yes, my friend Emma is among their number," Abigail answered. "They tell me they have longed to find a place they can truly call home, and when they arrived in Archangel Territory this was the spot that resonated as home. Isn't that right, Vasili?"

"You have got the story right Abbie," Vasili confirmed. "You've been listening well at our campfires."

Abigail smiled under the tattooed man's praise.

Raven wanted to punch something, maybe Vasili.

The men loaded the statue onto the cart and Vasili managed to find where they parked their steam coach. How had the gypsy found it? Was he Fae as well?

Raven sniffed at him, nothing notable but he could just as easily be masking his scent, his skills were sorely lacking in this place.

"Thank you for your help, Mr. O'Toole." Laurel shook the man's hand before her husband lifted her into the carriage. "Will you come with us, Abbie?"

"Yes, I think I will. Vasili, will you tell Emma I left with my friends?"

"Certainly," he answered.

Even though they got underway quickly, it wasn't fast enough for Raven.

After the Market on Saturday, everyone was exhausted so Monday morning was soon enough for Doc to see Abigail. The exam also gave Doctor Gunn a chance to utilize the new medical office which the miners furnished when they heard a doctor was going to begin practicing in the building again.

Raven was impressed at how still Abigail sat as Doctor Gunn poked and prodded her. "It's interesting you suddenly recalled Sophia Pembrooke's name."

Abigail pressed her fingers to her temples. "Could you rather not?" she asked.

"Just hearing her name inflicts pain?" Doctor Gunn asked.

"Yes." Her voice was clipped.

"I wonder." He rummaged through his bag. "I suppose this will work in a pinch." He plucked out his pocket watch and held the timepiece next to her ear.

Abigail went still as a stone.

"What did you do to her?" Raven's voice filled with concern. "She seems to be in a trance."

"She is. She's been hypnotized," Doc answered.

"You didn't need to do that." Raven didn't like the idea of Abigail being under someone's control.

"I didn't. Someone else did," Doc backed away from him.

"Doctor Pembrooke," Moody answered from the doorway.

"My suspicion as well," Doc confirmed.

"How? Sophia's not Fae," Raven stated.

"No, but she is an excellent hypnotist. It took a significant amount of power for Moody to undo the trance-like state she had positioned me in when I was under her charge." Doc sat in a nearby chair, his face haunted.

"We can't leave her like this!" Raven barked.

Doc startled. "Of course not. I simply wanted to confirm my suspicions. Let us give her a few minutes and then perhaps Moody can help."

"Certainly," Moody acknowledged. "So what did Abigail do or see to warrant such a drastic measure?"

"Good question, Scamp." Raven procured the page out of his pocket. "I suspect this has something to do with Abigail's delivery. Her chart states she dropped off a dozen invisibirds."

"What could Doctor Pembrooke want with birds?" Doc asked from the bench.

"Most likely she tortured them," Moody muttered.

"And last I checked she is no doctor. There was a shortage in Constantinople, she could've practiced there, and yet she chose to work in Laurel's brothel instead," Doc professed.

"Is this something you can undo, Scamp?" Raven asked.

"Perhaps, but hypnotism is something which requires more investigation," Moody said. "What do we know so far?"

"Well, whenever we simply mention Sophia's name, Abigail gets severe headaches," Raven concluded.

"But now she remembers," Doc said. "Perhaps we could simply treat the pain, and let the memories come forth naturally. Moody, can you remedy that?"

"I wouldn't want to, but perhaps the gypsy witches could. Their magic can often work better on humans."

"I could ask Emma…"

"Ask Emma what?" Abigail asked from the table.

"To maybe prepare a tonic for your headaches which come on at the mention of HER name," Raven answered rapidly.

"Why, Emma? Couldn't Doctor Gunn prescribe something?" she asked.

"I could, but I'm positive you've been hypnotized."

"Hypnotized? Abigail was incredulous. "You can't be serious. Is that even possible?"

"Oh, hypnotism is very possible. As part of a circus troupe, I've seen some of the best." Doc told her.

"And Emma's herbal treatments would work better than say... laudanum?" she tilted her head and pressed her lips into a tight line.

Tread carefully, Doc. She's not a believer.

"Her medicine would be less addictive and herbs have been shown to have other benefits the modern painkillers may lack," Doc said with such conviction even Raven was impressed.

"Fine. I'll visit with Emma tomorrow."

"Don't forget to mention you were hypnotized," Moody informed her.

"Yes, Yes," Abigail said as she quietly inched away.

Once she was out of hearing range, Raven asked, "Do you think Emma can help her?"

"Witch magic falls between human and Fae, according to my studies, her herbals would seem the most logical. If Emma can't help her, I imagine there is a gypsy herbalist whom she can recommend," Moody answered.

"I still can't believe Sophia is here. Do you think she followed us from Constantinople?" Doc said.

"To what end?" Raven asked.

No one spoke for a few minutes as footsteps were heard along the back hall.

"Ben, you have got to see the upstairs. This will make an ideal hospital if you should decide to use the space as such. The rooms aren't overly large, but we could add some cots to maximize space." Laurel paused in her monologue. "What? What did I walk into?"

"Sophia Pembrooke," Moody said stoically.

"What about that viper?" Laurel's lips curled at the name of the Prussian who'd worked as a maid in her brothel.

"Why do you think she's here?" Raven asked. Perhaps Laurel would have some insight.

"I think she works for someone in the Holy Alliance. I suspected it when she worked for me, and I believe it to be true now."

"You think she was a traitor?" Doc asked.

"Yes, Aaron didn't go off on his own, I suspect he had loyalties as well to the Alliance. His mother was after all Russian," Laurel said.

"I believe there were more soldiers with body modifications besides Aaron," Doc said.

"I agree, there were more when just Ben and I were in her so-called hospital," Moody agreed.

"It can't be a good sign if she is here. She was in the process of creating an army for Victorovich perhaps?" Doc surmised.

"General Victorovich was rather powerful and held much influence with Nicholas at court. Honestly, I wish I knew more about her."

* * *

EMMA PROCEEDED DIRECTLY to Doctor Pembrooke's office. She followed behind a large brass ostrich pulling a cart of fowl for the holiday at the end of the month. Normally she'd agree this was none of her business. But after Abigail revealed she'd been hypnotized by the not-so-good doctor, Emma suspected foul play.

She'd waited until the doctor left before entering the building.

She sensed something evil in this place, but the heavy darkness was not magickal. The energy felt almost demonic. She was not an overly religious woman, yet she couldn't help but make the sign of the cross before opening the door.

There were a large number of miners sitting in the lobby. Her hand flew to her chest.

They all looked at her in stunned silence.

Emma raised her hand to prevent them from deterring her from her mission. She expected someone to greet her since the clinics were nearly always open, but for Doctor Pembrooke to leave a room full of patients was abnormal. Emma was greeted by Lewis Fishman, who sat behind a small table serving as a makeshift desk.

"What can I do you for, Miss Flannigan?"

She got straight to the point. "Is Doctor Pembrooke in?"

"You just missed her. She was having lunch with Mr. Baranov."

"Seems like you have quite a line here." Emma nodded at the small overcrowded room. "Is everything alright?"

"Nothing out of the ordinary. Doctor Pembrooke is merely doing check-ups. What did you need to see her for?" Lewis tapped his pencil on the desk.

"Nothing out of the ordinary. I was just looking to see if she had any extra bandages and the like on hand. You know how the Clan doesn't like doctors. I just wanted to be prepared for any upcoming needs as my own inventory is getting low."

"Those supplies don't come cheap," he countered.

"I didn't expect they would." She reached into the velvet bag tied at her hip.

"Let me see if I even have anything to sell." He sighed, dropped his pencil, stood, and shuffled to the back.

Emma watched him leave and tentatively followed in his direction. She didn't see him and drifted along the long corridor. The doors were closed until she passed an office.

He wasn't there.

She looked down the hallway to see if he appeared and did not see him.

She scanned the room for anything to suggest ill intent.

She strode to the desk and glanced over it. She swiped a file labeled, "Miner Tests and Results." She was just about to abscond with the folder.

"What are you doing here?" Lewis asked from the doorway.

She dropped the folder and turned. "I was looking for you and got curious." She raised her arms and spread them in an arc towards her hips. "This is all so fascinating!"

"We don't have any supplies for sale." Lewis stared at her down.

"That's too bad."

"Be that as it may, perhaps you should check with the new doctor down the street." He pointed down the hallway to the exit door.

"Thank you. I will." At least he gave her the excuse to stop and tell Raven and Doctor Gunn what she had found.

* * *

THE BELL above the door tinkled and Raven looked up.

"Emma." He hadn't expected to see Emma not after they'd spoken with Abigail just this morning. He stared, an inability to think, and doing a double-take. Emma very much resembled Molly. He still found their similarities uncanny.

"Inspector." She gave a slight nod.

"Were you able to help Abigail?" he asked.

"Yes, although I think your doctor could have prescribed her something without adverse effects. I simply gave her some whiskey with willow bark."

"I'll let Doc know." His throat thickened and he turned away. He'd not been able to rescue Molly, and he would have to answer for that.

"I also stopped by Sophia's practice."

He swung back to command a view of her, "Was that wise?"

"It doesn't matter whether my decision was wise or not. Abbie is my friend and I'll not let any harm come to her."

"I agree wholeheartedly," Laurel spoke from the hallway leading towards the house.

Raven made hasty introductions. "Emma, this is Lady Laurel Gunn and her husband Doctor Benjamin Gunn. Laurel, Doc - this is Emma Flannigan."

"A lady? Shall I curtsy?" Emma's tone was bitter.

"That's hardly necessary, I'm not sure if I count as a lady anymore. Victoria is rather put out with me at the moment."

"It would be rather difficult for them to strip you of your title, wouldn't it, my heart?" Doc asked.

"I'm sure the queen can do whatever she wishes. There isn't anyone to gainsay her." Emma supplied.

"True enough." Laurel nodded at the gypsy.

"What did Sophia say to you?" Raven asked before the two women were sidetracked away from important things like Abigail's safety.

"She was not in." Emma glared at him.

"Really, Raven, where are your manners?" Laurel chastised him.

Too late, things were already out of hand. "I merely asked a question." He raised his hands to show he meant no harm.

"Fine." Laurel smoothed her palms down her apron, before removing it. She set the apron on a nearby table and turned back to her tiny audience. "I believe it is time for tea." After she'd spoken she disappeared down the hall.

Doc practically flew after her, his pace so quick.

Raven bowed and gestured down the hallway. "After you Miss Flannigan, I find it's best not to dally when Lady Gunn is serving. "

"You'd think I was in an interrogation." Emma huffed.

"You have that right."

* * *

A HALF-HOUR LATER, their stomachs were sated from hunger with cucumber sandwiches and shortbread cookies. Despite Raven's misgivings Emma and Laurel got along famously and discussed how Laurel had come to be a Courtesan, and how Emma had traveled via air ferry from Russia to Archangel as well as places in Great Britain they both had traveled.

Raven glowered at Emma. "Why are you here?"

"Raven!" Laurel admonished him by kicking him under the table.

"No, it's fine. After I tell you what I found, I need to get back to my caravan anyway."

"Go on," Laurel reached her hand across the small table and gave Emma a squeeze.

"After Abbie told me she'd been hypnotized by Doctor Pembrooke, and let me tell you getting that bit of information from her was like pulling a stubborn mule with a large cart, I suspected the woman might be…" Emma paused.

"A witch?" Doctor Gunn supplied.

"Yes. Or the like," she continued. "So, I went to her office, but I didn't want to actually see her, lest she cast a hex or curse on me. I waited until she left and then approached her office. I entered under the guise I needed medical supplies."

Doc tilted his head, furrowing his brow.

"I'm one of the few gypsies providing medicine to the people of our clan."

Doc nodded.

"I asked her assistant, Lewis, for the supplies and when he went to the back, I searched her office. She's doing testing on the miners."

"What kind of testing?" Doc asked.

"I'm not sure, and even if I had time to look at her files, I wouldn't know what I was looking at." She shrugged.

"Understandable." Laurel patted Emma's hand.

"The other two things I can tell you are her lobby was full of miners, downright scary, I haven't seen anything like that since I was in Ireland during the famine."

"Were they sick?" Doc asked.

"I don't think so, but they had just come from the mines and so were na exactly tidy. When I was leaving, I noticed a door in the back locked with chains and a heavy barricade. Not sure what was in there, because Lewis came from a different area altogether."

"Sounds like something needing inspection." Laurel nodded at him.

"I agree, but I'll have to wait until I know Sophia's going to be out for a while," Raven responded.

"She closes up every Friday, so you could go on a weekend," Emma supplied.

"Doesn't she live in the back of her office?" Doc asked.

"There's no house attached to her building. I believe she lives with Boris Baranov or stays at his house." Emma's brow furrowed.

"My, how the high and mighty have fallen," Laurel revealed.

"Beg pardon?" Emma asked.

"Nothing, my dear, I find it humorous Sophia once judged me because I operated a house of ill repute, and now, she is living with a man. She was horribly judgmental of my profession and my girls."

The last was said with such intensity Raven changed the subject, "What about her husband?"

"She has no husband." Emma looked at him as though he were daft.

"She died in Constantinople," Raven said.

"Yes. She was married to Lord Emory Pembrooke. Her maiden name was Ostwald," Laurel commented.

"After Doctor Gustav Ostwald?" Emma asked.

"I'm not familiar with him." Laurel looked at her husband.

"He fine-tuned the process for artificial limbs and clockwork organs," said Doc.

"Your heart?" Laurel raised her eyebrows at her husband.

"Yes."

"You have a clockwork heart?" Emma asked, incredulous.

"Not anymore. Mine was only temporary," Doc answered.

"That's not possible. I may not know much about medicine, but I know there has been no successful clockwork heart transplant."

"Let us say not medicine but rather magick was involved," Raven supplied.

"Oh." Emma assessed Doc, as if she was trying to ascertain what kind of magick was involved.

"Can we tell her?" Raven asked.

"My husband and I are Fae." Laurel simply blurted out the truth.

A rush of adrenaline tingled through his skin.

Emma stood up. "I'm sorry to have intruded upon you, Lady." She curtsied. "And you, Sir." She reached behind her to collect her shawl.

Laurel grasped her arm. "Emma, what is wrong?"

Emma tugged back, rubbing her fingers over the place where Laurel had held her. "I know my place, Lady Gunn. If you need anything, let me know. I'll make your presence known without revealing your origins. You and yours are not to be trifled with."

"Why are you so afraid?" Raven asked.

"I'm not stupid enough to interfere in Otherworld affairs." Emma looked at her feet.

"Then, you picked an odd place to settle," Doc mumbled.

"Yes, as we understand there are witches, shifters and even some vampires settled here," Laurel said.

"Shifters and Vampires ain't Fae. You do not trifle with the Fairy Folk. Every good gypsy knows that. Their retribution is harsh."

"Emma, we didn't know we were Fae, until about a year ago." Laurel implored.

"How could you not know?" Emma narrowed her eyes.

"My husband wasn't told to protect what he is, and my father is a human, at least I believe he is."

Emma paused in her retreat and looked hard at each of them. "You are what we call Faelings. Eventually, you become so diluted, you appear human and are relegated to the status of merely magickal or witch. If you had pointed ears I might suspect, but even that is no guarantee of your parentage. Most Fae do na disguise what they are unless they are verra powerful, dangerous, or an abomination."

Doc's cup cracked and fissured around his fingers before bursting into tiny pieces.

Raven's claws started to peak, at the contempt in the word, 'Abomination.'

"Best not to use that word," Laurel said softly. "Emma, we don't mean you or any of the humans in Archangel harm."

"Are all of you Fae?" she looked at Raven.

"I'm a werewolf." He prepared himself for the disdain at not being a full shifter.

"That's good," Emma said.

"How so?" Raven hadn't conceived a positive reaction. He was considered tainted among his shifter cousins.

"Werewolves may not be welcomed by full shifters, but we have a few in the clan so you are not unknown to us. Actually, I understand you met Vasili. He's a werewolf."

Raven scratched his claws on the table.

Laurel frowned at him.

"What? It's my house and my table," Raven sat back, his thoughts scrambled as he tried to discover why he was the villain.

"Fine. Fine." Laurel posited her hands up and gave a small nod.

"You know a lot about Fae?" Doc asked.

"Only the tales growing up among gypsies." She smiled. "Because the clan is descended from Faelings, werewolves, vampires, and other creatures we are not obtuse when it comes to our origins. We are rather able to hide in plain sight. I'm curious how you were able to." Emma looked pointedly at Laurel and Doc.

"My family is in the circus," Doc stated.

"That makes sense, humans don't look too hard there," Emma commented.

"My father was a pastor, a man of God," Laurel said.

"Or spawn of Satan," Doc muttered.

"The church has long been in cohorts with the Royals on demonizing Fae. I'm surprised you werena found. What Fae was yer mum?" Emma asked.

"Banshee."

Emma turned ashen and weaved in place.

Raven stood and gently guided her down to her chair.

"Banshee. As I live and breathe." Emma made the sign of the cross.

"What?" Raven asked. "What is wrong with being a Banshee?"

"Banshees are pure. There are no males. Females are gifted by one of five families. The O'Neil's, O'Brien's, O'Connor's, O'Grady's, and Kavanaugh's have kept them in servitude for years. Her full powers are passed on to her daughter. There is no half-breed." Emma fixed Doc with a stare. "Are you sure you are Fae?"

"Yes."

"That's impossible. No fairy can hold the love of a Banshee. You'd have to be a…"

"Gargoyle." Doc smiled.

Raven caught Emma just before she fainted dead away.

* * *

"SHE'S COMING AROUND." Laurel handed the smelling salts back to her husband. "Are you alright?"

"I'm fine." Emma sat on the makeshift table which had been assembled this morning in a room Doc dedicated to his future patients. She looked past Laurel and Doc to stare at Raven. "Are they truly banshee and gargoyle?"

"Yes, but they will not harm you." Raven willed her to quit trembling and relax. If she was this disturbed by Laurel and Doc, he couldn't fathom what she would think of Moody.

"I don't know how you can be so cavalier. He's marked for death and she follows it. " Emma spoke to Raven in a low voice, as if not acknowledging Laurel and Doc's presence would make them disappear.

"We can hear you." Laurel placed her hands on her hips.

"Can I just go?" Emma looked frantically at the door.

"You are well enough." Doc gestured towards it. He had every appearance of being offended, but Raven knew he was protective of his wife.

Emma hopped off the table.

"Emma." Laurel's voice cut through the silence.

She'd crossed the room and opened the door before turning back to them.

"Yes." Her voice was small.

"You must understand we mean the humans here, no harm. You are one of the few humans we've met who knows about our world. Up until last year, we were very ignorant of it. If you would be so kind as to keep our secret, we would be very appreciative." Laurel's voice was soft without a note of censure.

"I will, my lady." Emma consented.

The door closed with an abrupt click.

<h1 style="text-align:center">CHAPTER EIGHT</h1>

Abbie awoke on Tuesday with a new purpose. She rose from bed planting her feet and squaring her shoulders. Now she knew who tried to make her forget and she would discover why. One of the things she had liked about HER was they were both women of science. She found it rare to be able to share her thoughts with someone as curious about the world as she was. Abbie hadn't experienced camaraderie with a colleague since Sam left.

Though Abbie's father was an engineer and possessed math and physics knowledge so they could converse, he was at heart an explorer, which is why he traveled so much before finally settling down. Now, he explored the world from the safety of his library.

She'd donned her overalls this morning, planning to spend the day in her lab looking over the invisibird breeding and genetics to discover what SHE wanted with the birds.

Abbie slowed to a crawl as she approached the dining room. Would Raven be there? Perhaps she should have worn a day gown to breakfast and then changed.

She paused just outside the doorway to see if she could hear his voice.

"Honestly, I hope she'll reconsider coming to tea." Laurel's voice carried into the hallway.

"Do you blame her for being scared, my heart? It's not as if Emma Flannigan has met anyone quite like us." Doctor Gunn answered his wife.

What did he mean? Was Emma being snobbish because Laurel had been a courtesan? Abigail couldn't believe her friend would be so rude.

"I understand her feelings on the matter," Laurel paused. "I do."

"Then why do you push her?" Moody asked.

"I want us to all be friends for Abbie's sake," Laurel responded.

"Ahem!" Abbie froze. *The voice was behind her!*

Abbie turned slowly to see George looking bemused. The lopsided grin he gave tilted in the same direction of his bow-tie.

"Is Inspector Raven in there?" she whispered to George.

"Yes, he is." Raven's voice came from the dining room.

A blush crept along her neck, and blood began to pulse on either side of her head. She whispered. How had he heard her?

"Come on in, Abbie," called Laurel.

"Just a moment," she squeaked.

A familiar clink, clink, clink across the floor let her know Trumbo was also in the breakfast room, making his way toward her. She was certain blood was rushing to her neck and crawling from her chin to her cheeks, prompting her brass pet to check on her.

"Hello, Trumbo." She bent down to greet her pet.

He responded by running his trunk along the warm parts of her face and neck.

"I'm fine," she told him. "It's nothing serious. I will simply die of embarrassment."

Trumbo's demeanor changed. His trunk wrapped around her wrist and he tugged.

She followed, curious about her pet's intentions.

Trumbo led her to stand next to Doctor Gunn. He released her hand and grabbed the doctor dragging him out of his chair.

"What does he want?" Doctor Gunn asked.

"I'm not sure. I said--Oh." she inhaled sharply as Trumbo's intentions dawned on her. "Trumbo, sit!" she commanded.

Trumbo immediately released Doctor Gunn's hand and sat. He focused his attention on Abbie.

"What's this?" Moody rose from his chair edging for a closer look.

"Sit, Stay and Heel are some of his base commands. They override any other codes running in his processor," she informed him.

She lowered herself next to Trumbo.

"Trumbo, listen." She kept her command short.

Trumbo's ears flopped forward.

Abbie had his attention. "I'm not dying. There was a misdiagnosis."

Trumbo's eyes started to flash green, yellow, and red. The clicks and whirs were audible as he processed the new information.

She turned back to their audience. "He doesn't understand figures of speech."

Trumbo's processor grew silent. He swiveled slightly, facing the doctor, his eyes glowed a steady yellow.

Abbie was about to tell Doctor Benjamin Gunn Trumbo awaited his conclusion to add the data to his Babbage card.

"She's perfectly healthy," Doctor Gunn confirmed.

"Fascinating," Moody spoke in awe, before patting Trumbo's head and heading back to his chair.

Trumbo's eyes switched to green and he followed Moody.

"I'm sorry about my appearance. I was going to spend the day working in my lab." Her mortification at her earlier blunder subsided thanks to Trumbo's concern. Abigail circled the table. The only chair available was next to Raven.

"No worries. We all have a day of work ahead." Raven stood and pulled out her chair.

She sat and tilted her head towards him "Thank-you."

"My pleasure," he answered before sitting.

"So what are your plans for the day?" she asked.

"I'm going to interview some of the miners who knew Mr. Turner," Raven answered.

"Ben, Moody, and I are going to finish setting up the clinic," Laurel announced.

"Oh?" Abbie's breath hitched. She figured SHE would have monopolized the medical field. Regardless of what happened, she was relieved the miners would have a choice.

"Yes. Many of the Free Miners expressed interest in a second physician and donated items or offered to help build anything we might need."

"You are certainly welcome to anything in my lab you might want. I have some older microscopes, test tubes, and other laboratory supplies. Unfortunately, I don't have much in the way of bandages and the like." Abigail frowned, wishing she could help more.

"We've already talked to the Free Miner Quartermaster and placed an order with him. He orders for the General Store and the other non-consortium businesses," Doc added.

"And you? What are you working on?" Raven's voice hummed along her spine, making her lean towards him.

"I'll be reviewing data for the invisibirds to see why SHE was so interested in them," Abbie added with fierceness.

"Emma found out she's been doing some testing on the consortium miners."

"It's possible she tested the free miners as well," Abbie said before George placed a plate of eggs in front of her. "She was the only physician until you arrived." She nodded at Doctor Gunn before piercing her over-hard egg with her fork.

"I wish I could get my hands on that file," Doc spoke before sipping his coffee.

"I could find the file for you," Moody spoke without preamble.

"You aren't coming with me to the mines?" Raven asked.

She couldn't resist smiling. Every time he spoke her heart did a flip-flop.

"No. Those miners are decidedly uncomfortable in my presence. You will do better without me," Moody answered.

Raven sighed, "You are no doubt correct. Thing is, I'm not sure my presence alone makes them entirely comfortable."

"Would you like me to join you?" *Where had that thought come from?*

"Do you mind?" He turned a brilliant smile on her.

"Of course not. My presence might set their minds at rest if you aren't ready to string a noose around my neck for Cornelius Turner's murder," she reassured him. Yes. She would go with him to make the miners comfortable. The fact she would be spending time alone with Inspector Raven Clarke was its own reward.

* * *

RAVEN SAT rigid in the coach. He should've insisted they walk or meet at the mine. These steam coaches only had one seat. The processing panel consumed the entire front of the steam contraption.

He was uncomfortable ever since he'd sat down. Abigail leaned forward as she punched the keypad. Her overalls bunched against her derriere. He should've looked away, but she was far too delectable. He couldn't help but stare.

Raven shifted closer to the side of the coach. He was hard as cast iron. He didn't dare move for fear he might notify her of his masculine presence. He took off his Stetson and placed the hat over his lap. He darted a glance and exhaled as he covered his attraction to her.

"Are you cold?" Abigail rubbed his arm with her gloved hand. "You should have dressed in something warmer like I did."

A blush passed over her like a shadow. Before they left her house, Abigail sprinted upstairs to don warmer undergarments.

Wonderful, now he was thinking about what she wore beneath her dun-colored garment.

He moaned.

She rubbed his arm harder. "We will be there soon. I admit I'm surprised you are cold in your wool winter coat."

"I'm not cold." His voice was terse.

"Oh?" Her hand moved away.

How he missed her touch. The loss was just as well.

He didn't want her feelings hurt. "I'm just used to spreading out more in a coach."

"That makes sense. You are rather tall. Laurel told me you were uncomfortable with the brass pachyderms in Constantinople." She was so animated the seat moved beneath her and her limbs teased him with their fleeting brushes.

"That is an understatement." He crossed his arms, trying to make himself smaller. At least his hat remained on his lap.

She turned in her seat. "Why?"

When he turned to study her, she was so close he had to withdraw to view the whole of her. He could smell the scent that was uniquely hers, and her intoxicating pheromone simply made things worse for him.

Her mouth was parted in a half-smile. What had she asked him?

"I'm sorry," he said like a dolt. "What?"

"Why did the elephants bother you?" Her eyes grew wide and he was lost in their blue depths.

He slid closer to the window. Damn narrow seat. "The basket on top isn't nearly as stable as your brass animal coaches here."

Abigail scooted closer to him. Whatever for?

"Did you see the menagerie the night of the ball?" Her blue eyes sparkled in wonder.

"I wasn't paying much attention to them." He remembered her though, she should have been unforgettable, but he remembered everything from her blue eyes and her dancing freckles to her overalls, likely the same pair she wore now.

She leaned over, pointing out the window. Her reach gave him the barest glance at the swell of her breasts, "We are almost there."

"Thank God." He held his hat firmly in his lap.

The coach rocked, hitting something on her side, and careened to the left.

His hat fell.

Abigail clutched onto his shoulder with her hand.

He reached around to grab her waist.

The coach stabilized but she clung to him, nonetheless. She had to be aware of his arousal. There was no hiding his erection now.

"Thank you, Raven." Why did she have to use his name? When she spoke his name the last of his willpower vanished.

"Oh hell," he said before dropping his lips to hers.

CHAPTER NINE

*I*nspector Raven Clarke was kissing her! And what a kiss. She'd been kissed once before, clumsily by Malcolm when they were younger, but this was so different.

Raven's lips were soft. The softness was unexpected. He was a hardened man, with lips which pushed with delightful pressure. He hoisted her closer.

Abbie inhaled the scent of him, and she was comforted by his closeness. She clutched his coat between her fingers, the wool scratchy. Her bottom nestled against his...his…. Startled, she opened her eyes wide and backed away from him.

His hazel eye fluttered open and he released her.

Abbie fell hitting the floor of the coach. "Ouch." She rubbed her hip.

"I'm sorry." Raven offered her a hand.

"For kissing or dropping me?" She forced a laugh and her chest tightened.

"For dropping you," he answered.

She smiled at him. "So you meant to kiss me?"

"I didn't, but I'm not sorry for kissing a beautiful woman." He smiled back.

She accepted his hand.

The coach slowed to a halt before Abbie returned to her seat.

The door flung open.

Several people stared agape at her on the floor of her coach while Inspector Raven remained seated, holding her hand.

She caught sight of women huddled and whispering.

"Ugh!" Abbie could only imagine what they thought. She released Raven's hand.

"What's going on here?" Malcolm Jones asked, casting a scowl at Raven.

"I fell resetting the dials." She fairly shouted as she exited the coach with Malcolm's assistance.

"Are you alright?" Malcolm asked.

"Yes, I'm fine. I should have never stood in the coach when we were so close," she said. At least she was short enough that her excuse sounded plausible.

"You are always in such a rush." Malcolm shook his head.

Raven finally spoke. "It all happened so suddenly, I don't think there was any stopping once momentum took over."

She swung her head back towards him. What did he mean? Was he corroborating her story or speaking of their kiss?

Raven winked at her, before placing his hat on his head. The rogue.

"Ooh!" She stomped her foot.

The only thing which stopped their kiss was her shock. If she'd let him continue; only the fates knew what state of disarray the townspeople would have found them in. She zipped up her overalls lest people think she was improper.

She clutched Malcolm's hand a bit tighter before speaking. "I believe the Inspector is planning some interviews."

"Oh? Are you going with him?" Malcolm asked.

"No. I shall check on the canaries," she responded. She'd had every intention of smoothing things over with the miners before circumstances changed in the carriage but after his kiss and her mortification. He could fend for himself.

* * *

"I'll see you later, Abigail." Raven tipped his hat at her, before walking towards the office. He wasn't sure if she followed or not but he'd give Abigail Phelan whatever space she required. He pushed against the door, unaware of the ringing bell overhead.

Cameron Jones lifted his hat up. He leaned forward in his chair and shuffled a stack of papers. "Inspector? What can I do for you?"

"I wanted to interview some of the miners if that's okay." Raven kept his grip on the door handle.

"I see no issue," Cameron responded.

Raven paused. He still wasn't sure the miners would be forthcoming in their knowledge of Cornelius Turner or where the man's arm had been disposed of, let alone possibly sold.

"What is it, Inspector?" Cameron grumbled.

"Abigail was going to go with me to introduce me to the miners. They weren't inclined to share information when I tried to interview them last week."

"So it's Abigail, is it?" He leaned back in his chair, with a faint smirk twisting his lips.

Raven hadn't even considered the consequences of using her name so casually. "At her insistence, Sir." At least the statement was true.

"Stood you up, did she?" Cameron asked.

"No, Sir. She opted to check on the canaries." He stumbled over his words and began to sweat. He was like an untried youth in front of this man.

"Inspector, call me Cameron, or Mr. Jones if you must. For Christ's sake, quit calling me sir. I work for a living."

"Sorry, Sir, I mean, Mr. Jones." Raven was propelled forward when the door slammed into him from behind. He managed to regain his balance and move out of the way.

"I'll grab the paperwork." Malcolm nearly ran Raven over heading to a stack of cabinets. "Sorry," he said.

"No, I was just on my way--" Anything he was going to say was forgotten at the sight of Abigail.

She met his gaze and a flush passed over her features. She was so beautiful in her innocence.

He was a cad for having taken advantage of her in the coach. He wasn't sure what came over him. His driving needs were unusual. He was torn between protecting her and possessing her. Taking her was all kinds of wrong.

"What paperwork?" Cameron asked from behind his desk.

"Abbie wanted to know how the last batch of canaries did in the mines," Malcolm said as he rifled through the cabinets.

"Give her the charts and she can escort the Inspector down. He needs to talk to the miners." Cameron pulled his hat back down over his forehead.

"But Abbie…."

"That is fine. I can escort Inspector Clarke." Abigail took the charts Malcolm handed her.

"Wonderful. While you kids are in the mines, Malcolm can disconnect that God-forsaken bell." Mr. Jones crossed his arms over his chest and bent his head forward to nap.

The bell dutifully chimed, and Raven turned to find Abigail gone. He raced out the door and heard a grumbling, "Now, Malcolm." just before it closed.

Raven searched. How fast could one human girl move? He caught sight of her braid as she headed for one of the open mines.

"Abigail!" he called.

She stopped but remained facing the mine.

Raven raced to catch her. "I'm sorry if I upset you."

"You didn't upset me," she huffed.

"Clearly, I did something. Tell me what I've done to offend that I might correct it," he spoke with sincerity

"I'm not upset with you. I just don't like people talking about me or my family." She strolled towards the mine entrance.

He fell into step beside her. "And you think people are talking about you because…"

"Don't you think you kissing me was rather obvious to all of Alchemia?" She grabbed a pair of metal hats with lanterns off the shelf and handed him one.

"I don't think we were scandalous. Did young Mr. Jones say anything?"

She tilted her head as if in thought, "No. And he would be the first person to tease me."

"Perhaps our kiss was not as bad as you thought."

"Perhaps." She blushed as she looked intently at her toes. "I'm very sorry. I'm not normally so--"

He couldn't resist some teasing of his own. "Impulsive? Stubborn? Adorable?"

She smiled at him. "Thoughtless."

"How so?"

"I know you didn't mean to kiss me, and I took my wounded pride out on you." She carefully lit both lanterns before placing the hat on her head.

"Didn't mean?" Raven followed her lead.

"That is to say, I know I'm not attractive."

Raven gaped at her. "Who told you these lies?"

"I'm four and twenty. Still unmarried. There are no lies, just facts." She proceeded down the narrow tunnel.

"They may be facts, but don't discount the fact that I find you very attractive." He ducked down as the tunnel ceiling closed in.

She turned to look toward him. "You do?"

"It is one of the reasons I kissed you."

"What other reasons could there be?" She asked.

He couldn't quite make out her facial expression with the lantern glow consuming his vision. "I find I'm drawn to you, and I'm not sure if that is good."

"Because you don't want to be." Her lips clamped shut and her eyes cast downward.

Raven lifted her chin and noted her unshed tears. "Because you are innocent and deserve a man who is not tainted by his past."

"What happened in your past?" She moved away from his touch and wiped at the corners of her eyes.

The thought of revealing himself to her was like a vice around his chest. "That is a conversation for another time. Let us check on your birds." Raven gestured for her to lead the way.

It was far too tempting to follow her into the dark. The overalls should've been unflattering, but Raven found himself wondering what lay beneath the canvas material as the uniform bunched and loosened with her saunter.

They didn't walk more than two hundred yards before she turned into a bright alcove along the outer wall of the cave. Raven followed her in. Upon entrance he noticed a flood of light, coming from above. He looked up. Sunlight streamed through a window covering a hole in the rock ceiling. Angled mirrors cascaded light throughout the cavern. She removed her hat and blew out the unnecessary light.

"Amazing!" He took his hat off and snuffed the lantern.

"It is rather impressive. My father learned the mirror trick in Egypt. We utilize some of the entrances to light further down into the caverns. If we limit the number of lanterns in the mines, we can reduce fires or explosions." She spoke as she moved along a set of cages, carefully taking notes on a clipboard she'd retrieved from the end pen.

"What are you writing?" he asked.

"Their color changes. Rather than drag a canary down into the mines to die, I've bred them to change color according to exposure. Low oxygen, methane, or carbon monoxide, they turn blue; heavy metals a bright red. This cage here was the last set I brought over, and they seem to be doing very well, keeping their standard orange here." She tapped the cage with her pencil before making some notes. "When exposed to crystal dust, these canaries turn a lovely shade of pink."

"How do they turn colors?"

"Mostly their genetics and diet. When I was younger, I identified some canaries which had tolerance for low-oxygen environments. From there the solution was a matter of identifying their parentage and breeding to adjust their color. If you give an orange canary red food their color becomes redder."

"Yes." Raven had seen that among some of the ocean birds.

"When the blue canaries are in distress, their color gene is triggered as well, and they turn blue because they are fed blue food."

"Why aren't they blue all the time?"

"Their natural color is yellowish-green. They learned that by turning blue, they are immediately brought back to the surface and fed and returned to their home cage."

"So they could be tricking you, just to come home?"

"Though the percentage is small, I'm willing to take a chance on bird trickery to save the miners. Besides, I test them pretty thoroughly before turning them loose in the field."

"Don't you mean in the cave?"

"Just so."

"How do your invisibirds work?" Raven wondered at their magic.

"They aren't actually invisible. They reflect light by reflecting the color back."

"What did you breed them for?"

"I didn't, they are a double recessive gene and occasionally occur. I only had a dozen of them after generations of breeding."

"So they are an accident?"

"Essentially, yes."

"What did Doctor Pem—she want with them?"

"Doctor *She* was going to utilize them in her clinic to respond to patients. She expected they would be less intrusive than a monitoring brass animal, like Trumbo."

"Did you just remember that?"

"I did. It is weird. The very notion of saying her name didn't raise any pain in my mind."

"Perhaps we can explore why Soph--"

Abigail posited her fingers to his lips.

He was so dumbfounded, he stared at her.

"I'm not quite ready to risk hearing her name just yet."

"Understandable. Still, her reason for wanting the birds makes sense, but knowing her as I do, I sense something more nefarious is at work."

"Was she so devious, then?"

"Yes. In Constantinople, she was single-handedly responsible for taking the lives of four people. She turned Laurel's former lover into an enemy. He, in turn, murdered three of Laurel's friends. One was Emma's sister Molly." He wanted to tell her the whole miserable story, but it was not his to tell.

"I wouldn't have suspected her of anything so terrible but the reason she wiped my memory has me concerned." Abigail's brow furrowed.

"It would be nice to know what test she was running on the miners and if your birds had some connection."

"I suspected Moody was going to get those?"

"He will, but retrieving the files would be much easier if she was going to be out of her office for a significant period of time. Emma believes she's staying at Baranov's hotel but she's not sure."

"You could get them the night of the Baranov ball this coming Friday," she suggested.

"That is an excellent idea. I'll mention the ball to Moody." Everything was falling into place.

* * *

EVERYTHING WAS FALLING APART. Instead of going with Moody to investigate Sophia's office, Raven would be attending the ball, at Laurel's insistence.

"We must make an appearance," Laurel argued.

"Why?" Raven didn't like her needling him one bit.

"To draw suspicions away from my husband and son," she answered. As if her logic made any modicum of sense.

"You're new in town. I'm sure Baranov will not even notice you are missing," he persevered.

"That's exactly why we need to go. Besides, you don't want Abbie attending alone." She gestured to Abigail who quietly sat sipping tea at the table. She'd been quiet since they'd arrived at his office.

"Actually, Father and I don't attend the Baranov Balls as a rule," she said.

Laurel swung her head so quickly that Raven imagined her neck might snap. "You don't?"

"No. Papa doesn't care for Baranov's treatment of the Consortium miners so it's always been a bit of a protest, our not attending."

"Could you?" Laurel probed.

"I suppose I could, but I'd want Papa's blessing."

"What about Emma?" Raven asked.

Abigail shrugged. "As a popular seamstress, Emma attends most events where her gowns are worn."

Raven glared at Laurel, "Why can't you attend with Emma?"

"When everyone knows I am married, don't be silly, Inspector."

"There's a novel idea, attend with your husband and I'll go with Moody, and get the files." Why wouldn't Laurel see reason on a practical plan?

"Well, I suppose that might work if Abbie doesn't attend." Laurel tilted her head as if pondering a great dilemma rather than an event with ball gowns and dancing.

"That will be fine." Abigail lowered her head. Even Raven heard the forlornness in her voice.

"I'm sorry Dear, do you want to go?" Laurel reached over to pat her hand.

"Yes, if I won't be too much of an inconvenience."

He was a true beast. Truth be told he wanted her nowhere near the ball or Sophia Pembrooke's office.

"Then you should go." Laurel squeezed Abigail's hand.

"I'll ask Papa at dinner."

* * *

OVER DINNER, the group discussed the plan to go to the ball while Raven and Moody stole the files. Their plan was to use her small brass photolithograph- a turtle named Testy. Moody would bring the turtle to take pictures of the file and then Testy would print them back at Raven's office. After the ball, Laurel and Doc would meet them at Raven's office to review the files.

Abbie wanted to go to the ball. She liked the idea of helping her friends. Emma had completed the final touches on her peacock gown so she had something to wear.

"Well, you can certainly use our invitation, it's likely lying about somewhere," Professor Phelan said.

"Papa, with your permission, I'd like to go," Abbie asked tentatively.

Her father's head shot up from his food. "Poppet, I'm not sure I want you involved in this. This woman doctor has already messed with your mind. I don't want her to have another go at you."

"I agree, Professor, Abigail's safety is paramount," Raven's tone was quietly critical.

Abbie looked at him, bewildered. Whose side was he on? Did he think she didn't know she was at risk? Did he see her as some child who needed protection? No, that was unlikely, given his amorous response to her earlier. What then? It wasn't as if she was going to be alone with Doctor Pembrooke. Abbie would be in attendance with a ballroom full of guests.

"Actually, Sir, if you would be so inclined, your daughter's presence would be most helpful in disguising the true nature of our business," Laurel proposed.

"How so?" her father asked.

Laurel continued, "I understand from Abbie your family rarely attends Consortium events."

"That is true," he agreed.

"Would not Abbie's presence set tongues to wagging if she attended?" Laurel asked.

"I suppose. You plan to use my daughter as a distraction?"her father asked.

"I do," Laurel didn't deny her plan.

"You have gotten bolder as you've grown." Papa smiled. Abbie wasn't sure if it was in admiration or censure.

"I admit boldness was necessary these past years for my survival." Lines formed on Laurel's lips as she frowned.

Her husband reached his arm across the table and squeezed her hand.

"You understand my concern," her father stated.

Abbie wisely kept her mouth shut.

"I do, Sir, and I assure you, Abbie is like my own sister, I will let nothing happen to her." Laurel broke the chink in her father's armor like a knight in a tournament.

"I would like you to have some extra protection since you'll be down a couple of men." Papa was finally seeing reason.

"Are you implying I should pack weapons, Papa?" she asked, pleased at how detached she sounded.

"No, Poppet, but I will ask Cameron if his boy can go with you."

"That's not necessary, Sir, I will go with the ladies, I'm sure Moody can procure the records alone," Raven barked

"Are you certain?" As much as she wanted him to attend, she didn't want him to feel obligated.

"After all, he is a master thief," he responded.

Abbie found herself smiling at this turn of events.

* * *

THE MORNING before the ball Emma stopped by and did a final fitting on Abbie's dress.

"I must say it turned out rather well," Emma stood back admiring her handiwork.

Abigail gave a twirl before the looking glass, appreciative that her friend was blessedly talented. "It is beautiful."

"Would you like a top hat as well?"

"No. I was thinking of wearing my hair up, maybe some blue and green ribbons?"

"That would be lovely. Do you have someone to style it?"

"Yes. Laurel said her maid, Libby, could assist me." Abbie rushed through the words, barely able to concentrate.

"Are you nervous to attend the Baranov ball?"

"Why?" She regarded Emma with serious interest.

"Well, you will be walking into the lion's den, so to speak."

"I'm not overly worried. There will be so many people there. Boris Baranov wouldn't dare try anything."

"I had planned on bringing Vasili, but perhaps having multiple wer--

women in attendance without men to encumber us would be just the thing."

"Papa was concerned enough that he asked Cameron Jones to attend."

"Did he? Cameron would cause more of a buzz than you."

"Like Papa, Mr. Jones refuses to attend a Consortium function. However, he decided he could force his son Malcolm to accompany us in his stead."

"Well, the two of you should serve as the ultimate distraction."

"That is our hope."

CHAPTER TEN

The evening of the ball arrived without further incident or complication. Raven was nearly driven to madness. Ever since Abigail first appeared in her dress. That dress of hers drove him crazy all night. The peacock feathers swayed in a haze of color. He found it difficult for him to concern himself anything other than Abigail's bottom. He imagined taking her like a wolf mates his bitch and the image simply made his pants tighter.

The front was virtually as revealing. The swell of her breasts above the blue silky fabric and her neck unadorned, made him imagine his fangs sinking into her skin, bruising her flesh and marking her as his.

He stood near Emma and Laurel at the punch bowl, watching as man after man danced with her. The sights made his stomach burn and then harden. His claws peaked to cause damage, and his jaw hurt from trying to keep his canines in check. All he understood was my woman, my mate, mine.

"Are you alright?" Emma nodded to the claws gripping the fine crystal in his hands.

"I'm fine."

"You are allowed to dance with her," Laurel said.

He lifted his gaze, "I cannot dance."

"Truly? I reasoned perhaps in the Army..."

"The army was not concerned with etiquette, only results."

"I can have Ben or maybe Vasili cut in." Laurel shrugged before taking a delicate sip.

"The set is nearly done, you can simply collect her and take her out to the gardens, for some cool air." Emma made the action of retrieving Abigail sound so simple. "Go get her, man." To ensure she got her way, she pressed her hand Raven's back.

"I need to stay with you until Doc and Vasili get back from the card room." Raven wasn't certain Abbie would appreciate him yanking her from the dance floor.

"No, you don't," Laurel said.

Raven didn't know what he was doing but he couldn't help but move towards Abigail. He was drawn to her pure, natural beauty. Perhaps her innocence would rub off his sins if he simply stood in her orbit.

The set ended just as he approached.

He spoke just as the next suitor had arrived. "Would you like some fresh air?"

"Yes, that would be lovely." She gave him her gloved hand.

He led her out onto the terrace.

The garden was pretty sparse this time of year. The outside air was cool enough outside that perhaps she required a wrap. "Is it too cold for you?"

"No. I'm a native. I'll be fine for a few minutes." She spread her arms. The night caressed her skin. Raven had never been so envious of the dark.

"That is quite the dress. Emma did a wonderful job."

"She did. I like the bustle."

"I do as well." Or rather he imagined what was beneath the feathered tease of fabric.

"It took me forever to collect all the feathers from Norman, but I think the end result was worth the wait. Don't you?"

He nodded.

"I think I'm ready to head back in, maybe get some punch." She swished towards the door and pulled the handle. "It's locked."

He drifted along behind her and tried. Nothing. He tried two other sets and they were all closed. "Why would they lock the ballroom doors?"

"It may have been unintentional. Normally we don't have balls this late in the season. If we follow this walkway around it will reach the front of the house. And we can check other doors along the way." Abigail proceeded down the darkened path.

Raven removed his coat. He didn't feel the cold as keenly as she did. "Here." He placed the dark fabric over her shoulders.

They rounded the house before they found their first unlocked door.

"After you, my lady." Raven bowed as he held the door open for her.

He watched as she moved aside the heavy curtains and her bewildering bustle led the way.

Did she know how delectable she looked?

She couldn't. Yet she was the most beautiful creature that Raven had ever seen. "Do you know how gorgeous you are?"

She spun around her mouth in the shape of an "O". That small motion was his undoing.

He reached her within a few steps and grasped her around the waist.

He crushed her lips to his, trying to burn himself into her memory. How he wanted to claim this innocent woman.

She wound her arms around his neck and lifted herself upon her tiny toes to meet his kiss.

Their tongues tangled in exotic dance, and she learned the movement like an apt student. Her newfound skill was dizzying.

He lifted her and placed her on the nearest piece of furniture - a desk.

"Abbie," he hadn't meant to say her name like that, but Abigail seemed far too impersonal to him at the moment.

"Raven," she responded. Her dark blue eyes sparkled with humor and a bit of recklessness. Her legs naturally parted around his thighs and the skirt rose in place slightly when he placed her bottom on the desk. Her ankles peered out beneath the blue fabric and the alabaster ivory of her skin was so tempting.

He bent to place a kiss on the inside of her ankle above her kid slipper.

"What are you doing?" she asked in a strained voice.

"I thought my intent was obvious, I'm feasting upon your soft flesh." His smile was wicked and feral.

"Is that done?"

Her virginal knowledge drove him towards claiming her. "Even if it's not, I'm still going to do it."

He kissed her skin an inch or so above the last spot and trailed his tongue toward her knee, hiking her skirt as he went.

When fabric blocked his advances he used a claw to neatly tear the material. He kissed her inner thigh. He was more attentive, placing a lick here, a nip there until he reached the apex of her thighs.

The scent of her was powerful, musky sweet like liquor you savor warm. He swiped his tongue over her sweet lips, letting her flavor intoxicate him before dipping in and sampling again. "So sweet, your cunny," he murmured before he feasted.

* * *

ABBIE COULD NOT BELIEVE this exotic kiss taking place. What about this man that brought the wanton woman out in her? She never knew such pleasure was possible.

Raven lifted his head from beneath her skirts. "Lay back."

She reclined until she was horizontal, the cool wood against her suddenly warm skin.

He was lapping at her like she was a tasty dessert.

A heady sensation took over her, and each lap sent a warm shiver through her, like a current finding an outlet. She could feel the pressure building. "Raven, you must stop, something is wrong."

Damn, he did. "What?" He didn't even bother to lift her skirts, and his voice was muffled.

"I feel funny." She lifted, resting her elbows on the dark wood.

"Funny, how?" he finally peeked out.

"Wound tight, flushed, what you're doing, it simply isn't done."

"Says who?" he chuckled.

"Well..." she couldn't think of anyone who said such a thing, at least not directly to her.

"You are fine and what you are experiencing is totally normal. Let me give this to you." With that, he resumed back under her skirts.

She admitted to feeling a bit better, having admitted her feelings. She lay back again and tried to focus on her breathing, and how warm her skin was, but thoughts were dashed hard when Raven began sucking on her little pearl and tickled his fingers along her folds.

"So wet," he said before sliding a finger into her.

"Oh." Her hips bucked.

"It's alright Abbie, I've got you." His hand applied downward pressure on her hips.

He continued sucking her nub while plunging his finger in and out of her core until her muscles drew tight like a bow, and released.

Abbie moaned rather loudly, and bit into her palm to keep from crying out. Suddenly there was a piercing pain. She pulled away from Raven. "What the hell?" She placed her feet on his shoulders and kicked.

Raven skidded across the mahogany floor. He was stopped opposite the desk by a black leather settee with tufted brass buttons glinting in the moonlight. Blood dripped from his mouth and teeth. No, from his...were those...no they couldn't be.

Abbie's mouth was agape as she stared. Raven had fangs. The knowledge hit her like a punch to the chest and she was sure her heart stopped beating.

Oh No!

It was true...all the stories were true.

Her earlier bliss was replaced by a pain in her chest. She needed to escape! Abbie stood up, yanked on her torn pantaloons, and stumbled to the door.

"Abbie." Raven rose and wiped his mouth on his sleeve. The fangs were gone. Had those teeth been her imagination?

"No! Stay away from me!" At this point she was so terrified, she didn't care if people were ushered into the room. She would scream from the rooftops to get away from this monster.

No one came.

She stepped backward until she touched the brass handle and gave it a turn. She tugged and slid out between the single crack to freedom.

Once in the hall, her pace quickened, her kid slippers seemed to slide across the marbled floor as she moved at a rapid pace. She silently skidded to a halt upon entering the ballroom.

The lights were bright and patrons stared at her.

"Are you alright, my dear?" Doctor Sophia Pembrooke seemed to appear from the shadows.

"I'm fine." Abigail waved off the doctor, who she trusted no more than an adder in a basket.

She scanned the room looking for Laurel and Emma. They still lingered by the punchbowl. Watching the main entry for signs of Doctor Gunn and Moody. Abigail scampered as fast as dignity would allow, unheeding whether Sophia followed her.

"Abbie, are you alright? You appear distressed." Laurel met her halfway. Her friend clasped her hand before linking their arms and heading down another long hallway to the powder room.

Emma intersected their path and her booted heels clicked on the floor behind them.

Once inside the powder room, Laurel spoke loudly, "I must say, Malcolm Jones looks dashing in his formal wear. Don't you agree, Miss Flannigan?"

Emma held open the door and responded nearly as loud. "Oh, yes. I can't believe he is finally looking for a bride. She will certainly be spoiled, that one."

Abbie came out of her fog and was about to ask what they were talking about. The Family Jones would not be caught at a Consortium event.

The debutantes in the powder room seemed to fly and float past them like silk, chiffon, and lace dirigibles in an air race.

Emma closed the door with a click when the last girl had left. "We're alone now, tell us what happened."

"Raven...Inspector..."

"What did he do, Abbie?" Emma asked with such heat, Abigail was relieved.

"He bit me, he's a monster."

"Where?" Laurel inspected Abbie's neck and shoulders with gloved hands. "I don't see any marks."

Abbie flushed. "Not anywhere you can see."

Both ladies looked at her and each other before clarity crossed their features.

"Well, I'm sure his bite was unintentional. Do you need medical attention?" Laurel asked.

"Unintentional? He Shoudna have bitten her without her consent." Emma's countenance was thunderous.

"Will she turn?" Concern finally etched Laurel's face.

"No. I've never heard of anyone turning from a werewolf bite. Maybe with a full shifter."

"Werewolf?" Abbie began to wobble as frightening images played in her mind.

"Sit down." Laurel led her to a small stool in front of a mirror.

"You know? You both know?" Her mind finally registered their words. There was sourness in her stomach. She took deep breaths. She cast her eyes downward lest they see the tears in her eyes. She whispered, "I want to go home."

Emma bent down and lifted her chin, "I'll take you home."

Laurel's reflection looked as if she might protest.

Emma cut her off. "You need to wait here for your husband and Vasili. I've got her."

Abigail wasn't sure how long it took to get from the powder room to her carriage, but once there she looked hard at Emma. "Tell me everything."

* * *

RAVEN LET his eye adjust to the darkness. He wasn't sure what possessed him to mark an innocent woman except his own hunger to make Abigail his.

Was he wrong to want her, to think they could be together?

He truly did feel like the monster she had called him. Didn't he deserve that moniker?

He did. He truly did. To have claimed her without thought. Without acknowledging the consequences. He was a right and true bastard.

The door creaked to his right, and light filtered across the floor.

"Raven."

"Laurel."

"Are you alright?" she asked.

"For a thoughtless monster, I suppose." He couldn't get past the self-loathing he was feeling.

"What happened?" Bless Laurel. She could be so non-judgmental at times. At this point and time, her sound reasoning was the balm his soul needed.

"I lost control."

"Clearly, I would have expected nothing else to cause you to mark someone." She sat down next to him.

"She told you?"

"Yes, I think she…"

"Hates me, wants me dead, and wishes we'd never met."

"I was going to say she is in shock. In a matter of seconds, you not only took her innocence, but you also introduced her to a world she does not know or understand."

"I didn't take her virginity," he clarified.

"You didn't…what did…"

"I introduced her to a very intimate kiss."

Laurel's mouth formed an 'O' and she asked, "Well how'd that go?"

"Very well until I bit her."

"And why did you mark her?"

"I want her. Her scent drives me wild. When she walks into a room I swear I forget to breathe."

Laurel patted his thigh. "You love her."

He shook his head.

"You do."

"I couldn't...I'm not...I..." Raven thought. He had known Abbie less than a fortnight. Was it possible to love someone in such a short period?

Laurel rose and began walking toward the door. "I'll leave you to your thoughts. Don't take too long making up your mind though."

"So I can tell her before she leaves?" Was that puppy-dog hope in his voice?

"No. Because Ben and Moody will be here soon and we have to leave."

The door closed with a click.

Raven prayed he might get a reprieve from his dark thoughts when the door burst open and hit the wall.

In the doorway framed by light stood Vasili O'Toole. "I'm calling' ye out ye bastard!"

"Pistols at dawn?" Raven stood and faced his assailant.

"No! Claws at the caravan. Get yer affairs in order we meet next week under the full moon." Vasili gripped him by his lapels and lifted him off the ground.

"Why wait? Just have at me now?"

"Because unlike you, rutting beast, I have manners." Vasili dropped him.

Raven hit the floor with a thud. He leaned back against the frame of the settee and prayed for some modicum of sanity. Beaten to a pulp by Vasili O'Toole sounded like just what the doctor ordered.

CHAPTER ELEVEN

*A*bigail skidded to a halt outside her father's study. After all the amazing events Emma told her about last night in the steam coach, she needed to speak to the one person she knew would not lie to her. Papa didn't sugar coat or lecture. He would be straightforward and honest.

She took a deep breath before rapping her hand on the oak door.

"Come in, Poppet."

She peered in. "How did you know it was me?"

"George has an entirely different knock." He sorted his papers and leaned back in the leather chair. "I can tell you're upset. You have questions."

"How?" Her father's uncanny ability to read her was unsettling at times.

"Poppet, you have that look on your face. The same one you had when you'd learned where babies came from, how Trumbo's mechanics worked, and when you came asking me about your woman's cycle." Most people would've missed her father's brief shudder, the gesture was nearly imperceptible.

"I've spoken with Emma." Abbie's next statement required much more tact. How to broach the subject?

"Just come out with it," He waved his hand in a circular motion.

"Papa, she says fairies are real."

87

"Oh dear." Her father took a handkerchief from his pocket and wiped his brow. "I was worried about this day."

"You knew? How could you not tell me?" She exclaimed as she jumped to her feet.

"When? When was I supposed to tell you? This world is not an easy thing to reveal."

"I would think moving to Alchemia would've been the first real opportunity since this place seems to be a fairy Mecca." She paced the room. Suddenly Papa's expansive office seemed small.

"Sit back down. There was no guarantee that you would ever know who was Fae and who was not. I mean perhaps if you'd married one of the Jones boys."

Ignoring his request, she crossed her arms in front of her chest. "The Jones are Fae?"

"No, they are shifters. That is a different thing altogether." He made a dismissive gesture.

"Papa, I had an incident with a werewolf at the ball last night." Abbie heard the bitterness in her voice spill over.

"Inspector Raven?" There was a curve at one corner of his mouth, as if he was fighting back a smile.

"It doesn't matter who it is. The point is that I should not have been in the dark about this. What if something serious had happened?" she demanded.

He winced at her tone." This is exactly why I didn't want you to go to the Baranov Ball," he said in a low controlled voice.

"Are the Consortium members supernatural too?" Just when she believed she was gaining answers another question would pop into her head.

"I don't know, since I never attend the events." He crossed his arms in front of his chest.

"There's something you're not telling me," Abigail's voice rose.

"Did Emma tell you about witches?"

"There are witches too?" Her head was mystified by new perceptions.

"So, she conveniently left that part out." He sighed. "Emma herself is a witch."

"Is she?" Abbie was stunned.

"Well she's a gypsy, and they are magickal by birth."

"Bloody Hell! Are there any humans in Alchemia?"

Her father raised a brow at her language.

"Sorry, Papa." Abbie looked down at her folded hands when a realization struck her. "Are we human?"

It was her father's turn to glance away, "About that… Why don't you have a seat, Poppet."

* * *

ABIGAIL PHELAN WAS A WITCH. Her mother had been a witch. Abbie's maternal family traced their lines all the way back to Salem. At least, according to the ancestry chart in front of her on the library table.

After informing Abbie of her status, her father revealed to her a hidden panel on one of the columns in the library. In the panel were her mother's journals and a grimoire. Abbie was so taken at the sight of her mother's handwriting, she'd nearly forgiven Papa for not sharing her birthright sooner. She suffered a dull ache in her chest. She had not known the woman who penned the words before her.

"All the books about fantastical creatures from dragons to werewolves were acquired by your mother," he said.

"Or gifts," she recalled a few with inscriptions from her father to her mother, and it now made sense.

"Well, I'll leave you to explore."

Abigail poured over her mother's journals. She didn't know her mother, so reading the words she'd written was a connection she'd not known she was missing until she tenderly touched the pages.

She was so engrossed she didn't hear Moody approach until he was nearly on top of her. Trumbo's brass clinking gave the young man away.

She folded the journal shut, thrust the book off to the side, away from the doorway, and covered it with her family tree.

He followed her movements but said nothing about the books. "We missed you at breakfast this morning."

"I needed to rest." She didn't want to discuss her newfound treasure. "How did the file heist go?"

"We were able to get them easily enough, and your brass turtle was very helpful and efficient."

"Good. He doesn't have as much personality as Trumbo, but he seems to pride himself on being quick. It's as if he knows his natural counterpart is known for being slow." She couldn't help but smile.

"Actually the files are why I wanted to talk to you. There are some anomalies in them that we are unable to decipher."

"Oh?" Problem-solving was the one thing that could drag her away from her current obsession.

"The science is sound, but she's got what appears to be breeding charts in the files." His eyebrows raised in question.

"That sounds unusual for a case file," she agreed. "I'm done here. I can come and take a look." Her stomach chose that moment to growl.

"Would you like to review them over at the dining room table? I have to fetch the files anyway."

"Why don't you bring them back here? I'll clear this away and send Trumbo with an order to the kitchen."

"Wonderful. I'll be back in a few minutes." He gave an impersonal nod and strode towards the door.

Abigail gave Trumbo an order for the kitchen and placed her mother's journals, chart, and spell book back on its shelf behind the hidden panel.

* * *

ABIGAIL WAS ALREADY SEATED ENJOYING a spot of tea with her croissant by the time Moody returned.

"Is that stack in any sort of order?" she asked between bites.

"They were filed alphabetically, but I further subdivided them."

"How so?" She set her cup down on the table.

Moody placed the files on the table. "I categorized these by Consortium Miners, Free Miners, and Caravan Gypsies. Trumbo will be bringing the others shortly."

"That's interesting. To what end?"

"I was looking for any patterns among the group, but have been unsuccessful so far."

The files stared back at her. So much information, so much unknown. She gripped the table overwhelmed by the burden of secrets thrust upon her. How had she not known any of this? How could she have been so blind?

"I heard about what happened last night," he said tentatively.

She stood, toppling the chair behind her. "Does the whole bloody town know?"

"I don't think so. I only know because Vasili challenged Raven to a fight at the caravan camp." He approached her with caution.

"That's not fair. Raven will kill Vasili. I doubt a flesh-and-blood man can beat a werewolf." Abigail was a bit like Alice in Wonderland. Her whole world had changed overnight.

"No. A man cannot, but Vasili is a werewolf, too."

"He is?" She was caught off guard by this news. After what Papa told her, she should've suspected something, but Vasili never gave any indication he was a monster.

"Are you okay?" Moody righted the chair and offered her seat back.

She waved off his question. "When?"

"Next Friday night under the full moon."

"Is this fight going to be a spectacle? Everyone in attendance?" Panic raced through her as she imagined the entire town knowing her shame. She sat back down, trying to still her beating heart and regain her breath.

"No. I'm only going as Raven's second."

"Are you a werewolf too?" What was she to make of his young man? She had developed a brotherly affection towards him and now he may not even be human. She grimaced. Of course, she wasn't exactly human either.

"No, I'm something else." He took a seat next to her.

"Don't want to scare me?" She ignored the taunting voice in her head asking, *Why?*

"Something like that. I've been studying the fantastical for quite some time. You are only just learning of the world beneath this one." He touched her arm.

She found his gesture warm and comforting. "So you'll tell me when I'm ready?"

He seemed as if he might say something, yet after a moment's pause he appeared to change his mind. "Yes. Let's get back to Doctor Sophia's files and see what we might learn. The reason I separated out the gypsies is that we know most, if not all, are supernatural. I'm not sure if Sophia is aware of that fact."

"That is a good idea. Could you have Doctor Gunn do samples of your blood as well?" She wanted as much information as they gathered all the pieces together.

"He already did. He and I met Laurel when she came back from the ball and I believe he plans to corner Raven today," he said with a smile.

"Does the Inspector not like needles?" The corners of her mouth tipped upward. Imagine the big bad werewolf afraid of tiny needle.

"I'm not sure. I think the issue is more with what Raven did to you. He is avoiding Ben."

"Oh?" Rather than dwell on the events of the previous night or those ahead, she decided to grasp today's proverbial bull or rather today's unicorn by the horn. "Let's take a look at these."

As the evening wore on, Abbie and Moody laid out the gypsy folders and sorted them by category of Fae and shifters. Unfortunately, they didn't get very far.

"There's not enough information here. And these metal tests don't make any sense." Abbie groaned looking at the files.

Moody was sorting through the files in the howdah on Trumbo's back, "What do you mean."

"Without knowing why Doctor Pembrooke was testing these patients, or why she required invisibirds, I can't even tell if they are connected."

"We can run our own tests." Moody's optimism, usually contagious, was too much.

Abbie lay her head in her hands feeling convinced they would never connect Sophia Pembrooke and Cornelius Turner.

* * *

Saturday evening, Sophia Pembrooke sat in her office, reviewing the test results from the latest batch of miners. She'd placed the blood of the miners in the rats via syringe, but the results were inconclusive. She'd started with Mercury and Lead, but those proved fatal to the rats named, "Ostwald" that she injected with her own blood. The latest Copper and Zinc tests didn't kill the rats with human blood, but the metals didn't seem to affect those she believed had Fae blood either. She had promising results with silver, killing the Vasili rat, but none of the other gypsy rats seemed affected. The Ben rat had so far lived through all the tests.

If only she had a larger sample. Only a few of the gypsies had come to her for medical attention, and she wasn't sure how many of the consortium miners were even Fae.

The chains rattled on the door down the hall. She supposed she should check on Emory.

Sighing, she rose from the desk and made her way down the hall. She took the keys off her hip and unlocked the padlock.

Emory took a step back when she entered.

"Hungry!" He pointed to his mouth.

"I'm sure you are." She looked beyond him. "How about our guest?"

"Sleep. Long."

"She's not feeling well and still healing from her injuries." Sophie crossed over to the cot and placed her hand on her patient's forehead. "She's still very warm."

"Sick." He whimpered and tightly hugged himself.

Sophia saw Emory edging toward the door ready to grip the edge.

"No!" She reached her hand into her pocket.

In seconds, Emory seemed to debate whether to listen to her command. He ran through the open doorway.

Sophia pursued him. She raised her hand high, holding the switch that would stop him. She pressed the button.

The signal hit the electrodes on the collar around his neck. Electricity coursed through his anatomy.

Emory dropped to his knees.

Sophia didn't release the button until she stood in front of him.

Emory fell forward resting on his palms, panting.

She knelt in front of him and placed her hands on his shoulders before soothing him, skimming her hands down his arms before enclosing his left hand with his wedding band - matching the one on her ring finger. "Why do you make me hurt you?"

"Sorry." Emory Pembrooke wrapped his arms around himself.

"Let's get you some food and then you can go back to your room." She placed the control back in her pocket and stood.

Emory rose. He looked worried. "Girl. Sick."

"She can't make you sick. You helped a lot by getting her that arm."

"Good." he smiled.

"Very good boy, indeed." Sophia offered her hand and led him back to the small kitchen.

CHAPTER TWELVE

The moon rose above the makeshift arena composed of colorful caravans. Raven and Moody had walked from Raven's office in town. Alchemia was closer to the gypsies' camp than the Phelan estate.

They wound their way through the wagons, horses, and travelers to reach the outline of the circle.

"Over there." Moody pointed to where Vasili and Emma stood close to the middle in a square.

Vasili was seated nearly nude in the corner of a square of about four-and-twenty feet, surrounded by wooden stakes and rope made of hemp.

"You two go over there." Emma, dressed in a black blouse, matching trousers and a full white apron covering her nearly to her knees, met them at the rope. She pointed to the opposite corner. "We are waiting for Vasili's second. You might as well strip and give me your colors."

"Colors?" Moody asked. "We didn't bring any."

"No worries. I wondered if that might be the case." She fished through her apron pocket and gave Raven a fabric of blue material.

He recognized the scrap material from Abigail's dress from the night of the ball. Had he been such a beast? Was Abigail harmed by their encounter? He hadn't seen her since that night. "Is this from…?"

"No, it's material left over from when I made the dress," Emma assured him.

By the time Raven stripped to his smalls and Moody had gotten him some water, sponges, and towels, Vasili's second arrived.

Emma went to the center of the ring.

Vasili and his second followed.

Raven and Moody joined them.

Emma made introductions, "Drake Vermillion is Vasili's second."

The dark-haired man with pale skin began extending his hand. "Drake, this is Raven Clarke and his second Moody…what is your last name?"

"Jinn, Ma'am."

"Djinn, bloody djinn? That hardly seems fair." Drake took a step back. "He could kill me."

"What does it matter to you, Mr. Vermillion?" Moody asked.

"I'm a vampire. I'd rather not be burned," Drake said.

"But won't you heal?" Moody's pointed questions overtook his good manners.

"That is beside the point. Vasili, you will have to find another second. Maybe Sam?"

"Sam is not here," Vasili grumbled.

Emma held up her hand. "Drake, I don't believe you will have to fight unless Vasili bows out before the fight. Are you bowing out, Vasili?"

"No," he said with quiet insistence.

"Good. Drake and Mr. Jinn are here to ensure the health and safety of their fighters and relative fairness."

"Fine." Drake crossed his arms and proceeded to his corner.

"What rules are we following? London prize or Marquess Queensbury ring rules?" Raven asked.

"Neither. We fight by the Clan Caravan Commands." Vasili curled his lips before sauntering to his corner.

"I'll go over the rules before the fight. Pay close attention, as the crowd likes to participate."

"In the fight?" Raven began wondering what he agreed to.

"Only if they're lucky," she chuckled, "They will issue the rules as well. You'll see."

Raven went to his corner and Moody followed him.

Men and women came out of their homes and wandered closer to the ring. Children along with their caretakers could be seen sitting in the arena's wooden benches or on their caravans. Many waved red flags indicating Vasili's colors and their support.

He looked to see the dark blue material of Abigail's dress, flying high on the center rope stake opposite Vasili's. If fabric was any indicator he was not loved.

Emma picked up a bullhorn and turned towards the crowd. "Welcome, my friends and family!"

The clan yelled and whooped.

"And guests." Emma nodded to miners starting to fill the arena as well. "I'm your referee Emma Flannigan. I have the final say on this fight and will declare the champion. You are here to bear witness to this clan duel between Vasili O'Toole in this corner."

The crowd cheered, "Vasili! Vasili!"

"And in this corner, Inspector Raven Clarke."

"Boo!"

"Calm down people, let's get down to brass tacks."

"Just the brass tacks, Mum!" the gypsies repeated.

Emma began "Foul fighting is allowed."

"Or there wouldn't be this crowd!" the attendees answered.

She continued, "Kicking, gouging eyes, tearing the flesh, biting, Head butting, kicking a man when down is all allowed, but not below the belt"

"That's uncalled for!" The women laughed.

"Come close if you dare! Hang on the Ropes, but have a prayer."

"The fighters, they don't care!" The men shouted.

Emma asked, "And if the law comes to call?"

"They better be ready to brawl!" A few of the men took imaginary swings.

"All right Gentlemen! This shall be a brutal, fall-down fight, and then a battle pint!" Emma called out.

The gypsies cheered. "Fight and a Pint! Fight and a Pint!"

The loud cries indicated Abbie arrived too late. The fight had started. She'd much to consider in the past few days, including her feelings for Raven. Abbie knew she loved him.

She didn't want anyone injured defending her so-called honor. She overheard George telling Libby and Omar that these supernatural duels could be fought to the death. And while she understood the clan's need to protect her, Vasili included, no one deserved to die.

She propelled against members of the crowd.

There was little give.

"Excuse me!" Abbie elbowed one of the patrons.

"Ouch." The man moved a bit.

She squeezed through the space.

She elbowed the next body.

This man turned to her. "Hey girlie, this fight ain't any place for a lady," he said looking her up and down.

"I'm no lady, let me through," she insisted.

He widened his stance and blocked her.

"So be it." With that, she stepped on his foot with her heeled boots.

He hopped and lifted his foot.

Abbie advanced forward. She repeated this process until she was nearly at the front near the fight ring. Her tactics managed to propel her into the back of her last obstacle.

The man turned.

"Mr. Jones!" Abbie gasped and stumbled back.

"Miss Abigail Phelan! Glad you could join us." His smile was wide and full of humor.

"You are?" She looked beyond him to the ring, but all she could make out were shadows moving in and out of the lantern lights on the posts.

"Of course. Since these two men are fighting over you, would you like to choose one?"

"I'm not a prize to be won." She lifted her chin, meeting his stony gaze.

"Well you know we hardly let ladies decide these things." He was egging her on, she was sure.

"To hell with that!" Abbie stomped past Cameron Jones and froze.

In the ring, Raven was stripped to his waist. His chest, legs, and feet were all bare.

Her breath stopped.

Sweat gleaned across his chest and his muscles bunched as he swung a clawed hand towards a similarly undressed Vasili.

Vasili, the better pugilist, danced out of Raven's reach.

Both men bore the appearance of werewolves with their claws exposed and their teeth extended. Somehow Abbie formulated they would be more beast-like, but they merely looked unkempt. There the similarities ended and yet to Abbie the contrast between the two men was night and day.

Raven was tall and lean with muscles in his legs and arms, but nothing compared to the shorter yet bulging Vasili who had years in the ring.

Vasili punched Raven in the shoulder, knocking him off balance and slashing his claws across Raven's back.

Raven howled. He was losing based on the numerous slash marks welted across his skin.

Abbie couldn't see any welts beneath Vasili's many tattoos.

Raven's pitch-black hair had come undone from his queue, and he looked positively primitive. Despite his wildness, Abbie was drawn to him.

Vasili, whose bald head shone, reached out and grabbed Raven's long dark hair dragging him against his chest, and slashed his claws across Raven's abdomen.

"No!" Abbie screamed.

Raven doubled over and flipped Vasili off of him.

Vasili landed on his back. Using a claw Vasili reached towards Raven's face and cut the strap holding Raven's eye patch.

The patch flung off into the crowd who was suddenly silent.

Raven stood and stared out at them, "Have a good look, you bastards!"

Even she was not immune to his wound. She didn't know how he'd received it, but the injury had left him without an eye. Abbie was appalled. How dare Vasili embarrass Raven?

"Well, that bloody tears it." Abbie marched forward to the ropes. In a fury, she barely noticed the rope tangling in the fabric of her gown until she face-planted into the dirt.

Not even the wind made a sound. Though separated, neither Vasili nor Raven made a move to help her.

Abbie sputtered and spit out the dirt as she raised herself on her forearms. She kicked her legs and managed to loosen her skirts.

When she finally stood, the stillness set her on edge. The entire clan and some of the town were watching a new drama play out and she was the comic lead.

Emma approached her, "Abbie, get out, you can not be in the ring."

"No! They need to quit fighting." Despite the quiver in her stomach at the audience's attention, Abbie had no intention of letting this male bravado continue.

"If you don't leave Raven will forfeit," Emma told her.

Abbie looked past Emma to Raven. She didn't want to see him get hurt, but would her actions embarrass him further? Abbie considered his feelings for all of five seconds and decided his life was worth a bit of humiliation.

"So be it." Abbie strode to place herself between the two fighters.

"Abbie, leave!" Vasili pointed outside the ring. "Your honor is being defended here."

"My honor? Shouldn't I have a say in my honor?" She glared hard at Vasili.

"This is a matter between men. I will dispatch him posthaste," he continued as if he hadn't heard her. Perhaps he hadn't.

"Vasili, if you do this you are breaking my heart." She sensed Raven at her back. His hand came to rest on her shoulder.

"Move out of the way." Vasili took a step forward.

"No. I love him," she added with a smile of defiance.

Raven nuzzled her neck from behind.

"Are you certain?" Emma stepped forward blocking Vasili.

"Yes." She basked in the knowledge of her feelings.

"Do you forfeit?" Emma looked past her to Raven.

"Yes." He brought both arms around her waist, leaned down, and whispered in her ear. "Thank you."

Emma lifted the bullhorn and called to the crowd. "Raven Clarke forfeits! Vasili O'Toole is the winner!"

The crowd roared.

Abbie loosened from Raven's hold ready to leave.

"Not so fast, Miss Abbie," Vasili warned. "He needs to make what he did right."

"Right? In my book, it's right that you do not tear him limb from limb." Abbie caught herself scrutinizing the area for an escape.

"He needs to wed you." Vasili's tone was serious.

"Wed me? Wed me?" There was no disguising the hysteria that crept into her voice. "I can't marry him!"

"Why not," this came from Raven. "Because I'm some unnatural beast."

"No! That's not it." she turned to face him.

"Because I'm less than whole." he pointed to his socket.

"Of course not." She threw her hands up, exacerbated. "It has nothing to do with your perceived imperfections. This is about what I want. I get to make choices too." She stormed for two steps before a hand encircled her above the wrist.

Raven turned her toward him. "What do you want, Abbie?"

The tenderness in his eye was her undoing. She approached him, caressed his cheek, and whispered, "You! I want you, but not because society dictates we should. Because I made the choice. Is that so wrong?"

"No, of course not. Let me gather my things and we'll leave," he responded huskily.

Emma had swished behind them and gave Abigail a piece of fabric. The material was long enough that Emma had to reach to tie the dark blue silk around Raven's head to cover his bad eye and kissed him on his cheek. "Your injury seems to bother you more than anyone else."

* * *

ONCE RAVEN GATHERED his clothes and got dressed he let Abbie lead him away from the arena, uncaring his shirt and jacket hung open. Perhaps if he were human he would feel the chill of the night, but with Abbie nearby feeling any cold was unlikely. She set his blood to heat and he considered it unlikely circumstances would change even if he were a mortal. "Where are we going?"

"It's a surprise." She wound a path outside the caravans which led to a mineshaft, not in use anymore.

He followed her in. The tunnel looked to be a long canal big enough to fit the caravans in. "What is this used for?"

"The clan winters here in the mines."

The tunnel opened to a large circle surrounding a fire pit. Notches outlined the cave walls where the tiny houses on wheels might dock.

Raven could easily imagine the caravans lining the cave walls in a circle with gypsies gathered around the fire. "It doesn't seem large enough for all of them."

"This is one of five sites. Not all the travelers stay here, some travel south to warmer weather, but they have already left." Abbie tugged him away from the space until they came to a fork.

One tunnel was fenced off and the other open. She moved quickly and there were no landmarks in this place. Raven had no idea where she was leading him.

Raven wasn't sure how far they had gone until he heard birds - so numerous an individual song could not be recognized. As they moved further into the tunnel the gray cave rock gave way to bright colors of movement and a nearly deafening noise. As Abbie tugged him forward, the cages would change color as the occupants caught the briefest glimpse of their mistress.

Suddenly, the dark-colored stone cavern opened up in nearly blinding white. Raven found himself in the ballroom where he'd first seen Abigail.

The moon was full tonight, allowing natural light to filter through the glass ceiling panes giving the flowers, metal, and stone an ethereal glow.

Abbie released his hand. Her luminous white skirt swished in front of him, contrasting against the red brick path.

He pursued his quarry.

She opened a cedar door and gestured for him to enter.

He stepped inside. The hush white room had a small sitting area with two chairs and a table in one corner and a birch desk which seemed practical in the other.

"This is your room?"

"This is my office." She stood poised to open a cedar door next to bird-themed books sitting on a shiny metal shelf. "Back here." She led him past an opulent bathroom down a blink of a hallway to another door of stained glass, outlined in mahogany. The stained glass formed a patchwork of flowers and birds.

She pressed the handle and ushered him in. The room was bathed in the palest colors. A misty valley green stone lined the floor. A simmering ridge of flowers painted the walls. Looking up he saw the dark zenith blue sky dotted with sparkling champagne stars through a glass domed ceiling and in the middle of the room was a brass bed. Atop the bed lay a patchwork quilt of different materials and colors covered with pristine ivory sheets if the embroidery pillows were any indicator. The scent of lemon and lavender was heavy in this room which gave him comfort as the scent of his mate.

"You don't have a room in the mansion?" He needed to slow down. His reaction was to leap on her with want.

"Neither Papa nor I do. He has a hidden panel off his study accessing his own sanctuary. The house rooms are for guests. We prefer to remain with our work."

"Abbie," he stopped at her smile. He realized after their last encounter he was willing to drop the formality between them. "Abbie, what do you want of me?"

"Raven, I confessed my love to you back in that arena, I brought you here to show you."

"How very romantic," he drawled. Whoever said females were emotional and without logic had not met his woman.

"It is romantic, dammit!" She placed her hands on her hips and squared off facing him.

Her fiery temper revealed more than she might know. Her breathing had increased, her heart beat faster and he could smell her scent as the aroma besieged him.

Raven closed the distance between them, wrapping his arms around him. "You're right your gesture is romantic."

She leaned into him, pressing her small form against his hardened one. "Well, do you have anything to say to me?"

"Such as," he teased her.

"Ooh!" she pounded her fists on his chest, struggling to cast distance between them.

He held her tightly. "You do know that I love you?"

Her struggles stopped. "You do?"

"Why do you think I marked you? I want you to be mine in all ways."

"Truly?"

"Yes, do you want to belong to me?"

"Only if you belong to me as well."

"Absolutely."

He should have expected her exuberance, but he was unprepared for the leap into his arms, and when she kissed him full on the mouth.

Her lips pressed hard into his, and he recalled she was still new to the art of lovemaking.

He danced with her until her knees pressed against the back of the bed and she was forced to sit, breaking their kiss.

She stared at him and went back to his groin.

"May I?" She licked her lips.

He groaned. Was she asking what he thought? His breath tightened in his chest.

"I mean I rather liked your mouth on me. Would you like my mouth on you as well?"

"Yes!" Even he heard the plea in his voice.

He watched as she expertly undid his trousers, releasing his cock.

She feathered her fingers over his shaft before wrapping her delicate digits around him and kissing the tip.

He arched at her virginal torment. "Use your tongue."

She flicked her pink tongue out and licked the underside.

"Let me in your mouth," he commanded gently.

The touch of her lips around him was a delectable sensation and her mouth was warm and moist. She was a quick student and began moving her magical tongue in slow insistent circles.

"Abbie," he raised her chin and gazed into the blue depths of her eyes, he pushed her away before he lost himself. He shrugged out of his clothes and was mildly disappointed she hadn't followed suit.

She lay back on her elbows giving him a glassy gaze.

"Sit up," he compelled her.

She did as he bade, her eyes heavy with need.

His tongue traced the soft fullness of her lips.

She opened her mouth.

His kiss was slow and thoughtful as he used a claw to sever the laces at her back.

She inhaled sharply.

"I will never hurt you my love," he soothed his hands along her bare back.

She shivered beneath his touch.

He kissed the pulsing hollow at the base of her throat, before pulling her top down and exposing her perfectly formed alabaster breasts. Her rosy nipples were tightly beaded, and he couldn't resist a taste.

He cupped her bare breasts before dipping his head to one nipple and rolling his tongue around it.

She buried her face against his throat, her vibrating moans tickling along his skin.

He pressed her back against the mattress, trailing kisses down to her navel, tugging the dress as he went. As he slid the gown over her hips, the material covering his eye was caught and he paused.

"What's wrong?"

"I have to untangle my bandage from your skirt, it's caught," he warned her.

"Oh. Here let me help." She stood wasting no time untangling from the skirts confines as she shimmied and wriggled free. "There."

Unfortunately, she'd exposed his eye along with her nearly naked form.

He closed his eyes and let his hair fall over it, yet not before she noticed.

"I'm sorry." She looked appalled.

"Does it bother you?" he confessed.

She knelt on the floor facing him. "Not a whit." She combed back his ebony hair, pressed a finger for him to close his eye and kissed his eyelid. "It could be an infection risk if it's open, which is my concern."

"Perhaps." His throat swelled at her concern.

"Well then, let us cover it." She stood and moved to a dresser and extracted an eye patch.

"Whatever are you doing with that?" he asked.

"It's actually left over from a costume ball this past October. I was an air pirate."

"Were you, now?" He watched her saunter to him in nothing but her drawers, stockings and heeled boots.

She handed him the patch.

"Thank you." He sat down on the bed before leaning back. "Abbie, would you indulge me?" He gave her a wicked smile.

Her golden hair had come loose during her tangling in the ropes, the run over here, and the tiny amount of bed play. Blond waves hung nearly to her waist making her appear a seductress rather than an innocent maid. "Of course."

"Remove your pantaloons."

Her eyes flashed like sapphires as she raked an assessing gaze over him. Slowly she granted his wish by removing the garment.

His mouth watered at the sight of her puss.

"Do you approve?"

"Yes, come here," he growled feral, seeing his mark upon her thigh.

She approached like a doe did a stream, her thirst was clear, but what waited was uncertain.

"Abbie, let me give you pleasure."

The little deer left and suddenly she was more like a lion, unafraid.

"Straddle my stomach," he said.

She did as bid, and her wetness seared his skin.

"Lean forward,"

Her hips rose off him.

He lifted his fingers to stroke between her soft feminine curls.

She leaned forward granting him access.

He took a nipple into his mouth and sucked.

She moaned.

He probed his fingers back and forth over her slit until she was rocking against his fingers. He began lowering her down until he removed his fingers

"Abbie, lower yourself." he gritted out.

Her puss rested against his cock.

"Rock, darling."

She proceeded as she had before until she was panting heavily above him. Just a bit more and his mate would find her bliss.

He adjusted so as she rocked the tip of him would be at her opening.

Her enchanting blue eyes widened as he barely entered her sweet wet sheath.

"You set the pace, my sweet Abbie." He reached forward to rub her glistening pearl with the pad of his thumb while he nibbled on her pink nipple.

She cried out as she crashed down on him, hard.

* * *

STARS SHATTERED behind Abbie's eyes as she took Raven all the way. She was so full. She shuddered as she pulsed uncontrollably around him. She rocked on him until her breathing returned to normal.

He remained stiff inside her.

"Are you not done?"

"Not yet."

"Oh?"

"If you are too sore, my love, I can wait until our next encounter."

"I'm not sore but I feel very full of you. Is there more?"

"Oh yes, if you'll let me."

"Certainly." Granting him the same pleasure seemed only fair.

He lifted her off him and got behind her.

"This is different." she squealed with a fluttery feeling in her belly.

"Not for wolves."

"Oh." She wasn't sure how to respond.

"Let's get you worked up again." He slid his penis over her clit and began rubbing the tender bud as his fingers explored between her folds.

"Raven, that is so…" she didn't have words for the way he mastered her like a well-tuned instrument.

"You like that?"

"I love that," she surrendered to the fierce need he was building with her.

His fingers strummed along her folds, teasing and petting before he parted them and replaced his digits with his cock.

"Oh, yes."

He wound a hand to rub the bud of nerves working back to an orgasm.

He bent over her back whispering in her ear. "Abbie, I want to mark you as my mate, right here." He licked her neck.

"Alright," she was mindless in her passion.

"That means I'm going to bite you."

She should've been scared, but the idea of belonging to this passionate beast was appealing, she longed to be safe in his embrace. "Please, yes."

Once she surrendered to him, he thrust into her with abandon. she met each thrust and arched towards his exploring fingers.

He increased the tempo and she answered his thrusting hips.

She was seized by an intense sensation, she cried out with audacious abandon as waves of euphoria coursed through her.

Raven cried out before he bit the juncture between her neck and shoulder.

She collapsed.

He rolled off to the side dragging her back against him, kissing her neck and shoulder.

She didn't protest and sighed letting sleep take her.

CHAPTER THIRTEEN

Sophia Pembrooke reviewed the latest results and decided iron mixed with the virus would serve her best. All the rats with Fae blood had died with the exception of "Vasili".

Lewis scurried into her office, bringing more paperwork. "Doctor Pembrooke, I've been working with that flu inoculation, and I think we've created enough to inject the miners."

"I want to make sure we can immunize the townspeople as well in the event we have a breakout." What she needed was enough to kill the Fae, and she did not know how many were in this town.

"I will leave you these latest tests."

"Which metal?" she asked.

"Silver."

She glanced over the tests. Only one rat was affected. "You didn't put blood in the Vasili vial?"

"No. That specimen was part of the control group which only received the metals," Lewis answered.

She had informed Lewis she wanted to test the metals separately to ensure that metals in the mines didn't have an adverse effect on the inoculation or perhaps the miner themselves. The theory was plausible enough, and Lewis didn't question her. "That is interesting."

"Will you require anything else, ma'am?"

"No, Lewis. I only came in today to check on the latest test results. You may head back out."

"Thank you, Doctor and it was no trouble to come in. I'm always available if you need me."

"That is kind of you, but I assure you, I am fine." Sophia suspected Lewis had a bit of a crush on her, which could be a problem. She searched the iron tests for his name and found that his rat had died as well, along with Emory's rat, well too bad. At least the Fae flu would kill two problems with one cold.

Sophia stayed in her office, listening as Lewis locked cabinets and shuffled around before he finally closed the door

"About damn time," she muttered. She strode to the front door ensuring it was locked before heading to where she kept Emory.

One-by-one, she twisted the iron key in the set of padlocks holding the chains in place. When she opened the door, Emory was huddled in a corner, his knees folded to his chest.

"How's our patient doing?" she asked him, not truly expecting an answer.

He winced at her voice and ducked his head down, not meeting her gaze.

Sophia looked at the redhead lying pale on the bed. She'd planned to use the invisibirds to deliver the flu virus she engineered, but this girl would serve just as well. She had already converted Cornelius Turner's arm to retrofit her patient. A few additional modifications and the mechanism could release the iron particles into the air.

"Emory, would you like to be rid of your roommate?"

"Yes," his voice was muffled with his head down.

"Then you will have to bring her to her clan. Do you think you can do that?"

He lifted his gaze to stare at her. "Yes."

"Good." Sophia walked to the cot, and looked down at her patient.

Sweat beaded across her patient's brow and she shivered. Keeping a patient in a state of sickness yet alive was difficult. She leaned down and plucking a damp cloth from a basin on the side table wiped the girl's forehead.

"What do you say, Molly? Would you like to go home?"

* * *

RAVEN WOKE up with Abigail curled against him. He hesitated to wake her from her much-needed rest.

In the middle of the night after removing the remainder of her underthings, they made love once more. Less fervently, more explorative and tender. This was probably how one ought to make love, but his Abbie didn't seem to mind his beastly ways.

The sharp ringing sound of little metal feet on the stones indicated Trumbo's approaching. Raven decided to remain in bed. Best the brass pachyderm learned he wasn't the only male in Abbie's life.

Raven shook his head. Did he actually refer to a mechanical as "he"?

Trumbo clinked his way over to the bed where Abbie slept.

Raven noticed the elephant had a tray on its back with cups and biscuits. How long had they slept?

Using his trunk he nudged Abbie's hand.

"Trumbo, not now, Raven and I are sleeping." She nudged her bottom back into him.

He didn't mind her nudging posterior at all, but they probably needed to leave their cocooned haven. "Abbie, perhaps we have been in bed too long. Your pet has brought subsistence."

Her blue eyes flew open. "Oh, dear."

She shook the pastel blue covers off and stood quickly, he was impressed that her pet Trumbo hadn't dropped the tea and biscuits.

"What is the hurry?" He was curious as to her sudden change in demeanor.

Heedless of her own nudity, she threw his clothes at him. "You don't understand."

Trumbo neatly navigated around her as she haphazardly moved about the room in a whirlwind.

"So explain it." He loved this woman, but her sudden mood changes baffled him at times.

She paused before going into what appeared to be a small closet and turned to face him. "If he brought food, that means we've missed breakfast." She selected a white chemise and pantaloons.

"So." He shrugged his shirt on, fastening the buttons.

"It means everyone knows we are probably together," she sighed as she threw the white wispy fabric over her head and threw on her drawers.

"Why is that a problem?" Was she ashamed of him?

"Do you want to end up married to me?" She flitted to the closet, choosing a white blouse and gold corset.

"Is that rhetorical, or are you asking me?" He slid his legs into his pants.

"Rhetorical, you idiot." Her voice muffled as she shoved her arms in her blouse and tugged on another underskirt, before walking to him with the corset in hand.

"I see." As he suspected, she didn't sincerely want him, at least not permanently on an everyday basis. For a girl who said she loved him, at times she acted very odd.

"Help me with this." She handed him her corset.

"This goes against my nature, dressing a beautiful woman." Even though he dutifully helped her with her hooks and buckles.

Once the task was completed she walked back to her wardrobe.

"What's wrong with me?" He stood, buttoned his pants and reached for his boots in the event he needed to leave.

"Nothing." She turned her head to watch him, but her hands remained on the rack of dresses.

"Why don't you want to marry me, then? You said last night you loved me." Now that his socks were on, he kicked his feet into his shoes.

"I do love you. I didn't lie about my feelings." She'd selected a robin's egg blue skirt she was now pulling over her head.

"Then why won't you marry me."

"I'm not ready." She walked over to him and rested her hand on his cheek. "I want to be absolutely sure we would suit. I'm not some debutante looking to make a good match."

"I don't want your money." He was not a fortune hunter.

"Did I say you did?" She bit her lip as she buttoned her jacket.

"I have to go. I'll leave through the tunnels so no one knows I was here." Best he left before he said something stupid.

"At least have something to eat before you head off in a huff." She gestured towards Trumbo's tray.

"If you insist." He grabbed a biscuit before heading out the door and towards the tunnels, but was stopped before he exited the conservatory.

"Oh good, you're still here." Doc rushed to greet him.

"Yes." Perhaps Abbie was right and the household did know what had transpired between them last night.

"You need to come with me." Doc sidled up beside him and pushed on his shoulder. Doc didn't let up, riding his heels through the tunnels.

"Why are we going this way? Professor Phelan is back there." No doubt Abbie's father wanted his head on a pike.

"Whatever are you going on about?"

"I assume he wants to speak to me about Abbie's...consummation?"

"If he does, he didn't say anything about it, at least not at breakfast." Doc shrugged. "Be thankful he wants what is best for his girl. My father-in-law is a tyrant of the first order. I couldn't get Laurel away from that man fast enough."

Raven liked that others believed one day Abbie would be his wife, even if she did not. "So where are we going?"

"To the gypsy camp. It seems Molly Flannigan is alive and has returned to her sister."

Both men hastened their stride as they made their way up the tunnel. When they arrived at the spot where Abbie said the clan winters, caravans, and carriages had already filled some of the spaces.

"This way. My wife is over here."

"Do you smell her?" Raven was suddenly curious how other Fae tracked their mates.

"No." Doc paused. "I simply feel her pull on my heart."

Raven didn't have time to dwell on that before they approached Emma's brightly colored caravan with Moody and Vasili standing out front.

"What is he doing here?" Vasili crossed his arms.

"He is the only inspector in town," Doc answered.

Vasili blocked his entrance to the caravan.

"And I'm your only doctor unless you want to call that charlatan who has set up shop. Besides, my wife is in there."

Vasili remained motionless. "Don't care. You're na going in until Emma says so."

"Don't make me pull rank on you." Doc's face was red as he paced in front of Vasili.

"I'm not afraid of most Fae, including vampires, werewolves, shifters, and your djinn friend." He nodded to Moody. "What makes you so damn special?"

Moody stepped forward. "My father is a gargoyle."

Vasili grunted and scratched his jaw.

"And you're keeping him from my mother - a banshee," Moody revealed.

Vasili's eyes widened but he remained steadfast in his guard duty. Raven knew he was loyal to Emma and would not waiver. "I'll still be waiting for Emma's command."

Raven wondered at the relationship between O'Toole and the Flannigans.

"My heart, come out!" Doc shouted.

"What is the hurry?" Raven asked.

"She is in emotional pain. I don't want her to start crying, half these creatures could go deaf," he said.

Vasili looked at Raven.

Raven nodded his head in confirmation.

"Perhaps a knock on the door is in order," Vasili pointed out.

"Perhaps," Moody agreed.

Vasili rapped on the door.

The wood opened a slit to reveal slivered colors more vibrant than the outside, but nothing revealing the contents within.

"Yes?" Emma asked, one green eye assessing her guests.

"The doctor wants to see his wife," Vasili stated.

"Fine. I'll send her out." Emma shut the door.

Her action caused the scent of grease to fill his nostrils. The same smell he'd been assaulted with at Cornelius Turner's murder scene.

It was obvious he wasn't going to get anywhere near Molly, so he might as well start with the obvious witness. "Vasili, what are Molly's injuries, and did she return with mechanical parts?"

"Yes. She has a mechanical arm, an ocular monocle, and hearing discs."

"Interesting." Before Doc could ask more questions the door opened and Laurel tumbled out.

"Ben," she hurled herself into her husband's arms. Tears filled her eyes. "I can't believe she's alive."

"Neither can I." Doc hugged his wife fiercely and soothed her by running his hands along her back.

"What can you tell us?" Raven approached the couple. He needed more information and something was off in Laurel's scent.

"Let us talk back at the mansion." Laurel let Doc lead her back down the patch from which they came. Moody and Raven followed, leaving Vasili O'Toole and Emma's caravan behind.

* * *

INSIDE THE CARAVAN, Emma's heart froze and restarted. She stared at her younger sister before her. She wanted to scream from the top of the caravan, and yet also keep her sister safe and secret. Where had she come from and what had the Veil done to her?

At the sound of the door opening, she turned to see Vasili.

"How is she?" he asked.

"She seems well. But she hasna spoken and her gaze is unfocused like she is not truly with us." Emma looked beyond him to the cracked door.

"They've all left."

"Good." She sat on the bench attached to the caravan, letting her head fall back toward the wood. "I love having my sister back, but something isn't right with her. I may need to protect her from them."

Vasili grabbed a small stool and gazed at Molly seated on the bench. "I can help you watch her, make sure she's not a danger to others or herself."

"That would be very helpful, Vasili." Emma frowned.

"What is it?"

"We have to keep her arrival a secret from the rest of the clan." her gaze flitted to the other caravans.

"Why?"

"With so many of our family intermingling with the townies, I don't want the Consortium coming out here."

"Are you certain they even would?" he asked.

"I don't know. I can't be sure, Vasili, but I think that is Cornelius Turner's arm."

CHAPTER FOURTEEN

Raven, Moody, and the Gunns wound their way back through the tunnels to arrive at the Phelan Conservatory.

"I had no idea this was even here," Laurel exclaimed.

"I found this path the first day," Moody bragged.

"You could've at least shared this knowledge the day we went to retrieve the Gargoyles." Doc chimed in.

"I wasn't sure if this was a secret tunnel or not, as I'd never seen Abigail use it," Moody exclaimed.

"Fine, fine, carry on." Laurel tilted her head before shaking it.

Raven followed the family as they entered the archway of the conservatory.

Abbie stepped forward to greet them. "I was coming to find you."

"What did you need?" Raven asked.

"Not you." She turned to face Doc. "I've found something in the blood work."

They navigated in and out of plants before she led them up a spiral staircase which opened a panel just outside the library.

"Do all secret passages lead to the conservatory?" asked Moody.

"Yes or the tunnels. Papa likes to have alternate means of escape. The Consortium makes him nervous."

Raven nodded his head he had not been in Archangel long, but even he knew the Russian Mining Company was a force to be reckoned with. "What did you find?"

"Using my sanguine meter with some Babbage cards I was able to discover some anomalies in your blood samples."

"Such as?" Doc's gaze held focus as he moved closer to Abbie, forcing Raven to give up his position next to her.

"Let's have a spot of tea first," She said, walking to the sideboard and grabbing some cups. She placed one in front of each chair. "Please be seated."

They sat looking at one another. "Well, where is the tea?" Doc raised his eyebrows before he pinched the bridge of his nose.

"Trumbo should be along with tea and biscuits shortly," Abbie answered.

No sooner had she spoken when Trumbo arrived with two pots and biscuits on his back.

Once the tea had been poured, Raven spoke up. "The test results?"

"First, I know Raven is a werewolf, but are the rest of you faeries as well?"

They each nodded.

"That affirms my suspicions," She reached in and distributed papers. "I don't know what kind of supernatural creatures you are, but as you can see I suspect the results may be determined by the iron in your blood."

"Who is this human at the top of the page?" Raven asked.

"I used Papa as I'm reasonably certain he has no fairy family." she smiled. "I've listed the rest of you by name, along with certain other people I suspect may be supernatural, and the number below is your Hunefeld level indicating iron in your blood."

They all looked at the pages.

"As you can see Papa has a level of sixteen point five."

"That is pretty normal considering his age," Doc concluded.

"That was my thought. As you can see my level is eleven point nine which is barely outside the normal range for a woman my age."

"Low or High?" Raven asked.

"Low. Yours and Vasili's are at nineteen point nine and twenty respectively."

"My level is five," Laurel said, "And Ben? Ben is zero. Is that correct?"

"I ran his blood twice and came up with that result. You may run it again Doctor Gunn or perhaps you'd like to run your own tests."

Doc shook his head, "And Moody's number is seventeen, which falls within the normal range for a human."

"I suspect that Moody is not affected by iron?" Abbie asked.

"I'm a djinn. Brass is my Achilles heel," Moody confirmed...

"So perhaps shifters are immune to iron?" Laurel hypothesized.

"I don't believe so, I checked the Jones family."

"They're shifters?" Raven's heightened senses and possessiveness of Abbie around Malcolm was starting to make sense.

"Yes, bears, so maybe iron affects wolves differently," Abbie answered.

"Werewolves." Moody corrected.

"What is the difference?" Abbie asked.

Raven spoke up. "Werewolves are tainted. Unable to fully shift."

"Wow. How fascinating." No repulsion crossed her features, simply questions he saw stacking up behind her eyes. No wonder he was in love with this woman.

"What do you think your Hunefeld tests mean?" asked Laurel.

"I think Doctor Pembrooke was trying to determine what weaknesses were present in Archangel's fairy population. Or perhaps who wasn't human. I'm not certain. But, based on her testing metals against blood and the family lineages she'd drawn up it is my best guess."

"I would say your hypothesis is an accurate summation," Doc spoke up after reviewing the paper.

Raven added, "I wonder if she's planning on using your invisibirds somehow."

"Oh, I hadn't thought of that. I will run tests right away on the canaries to see if they have higher iron or other metals."

"What could that woman be up to?" Laurel hissed.

"I'm not sure. but I need more to go on than simply thinking she did something. Even Doctor Pembrooke isn't strong enough to tear the arm off of Cornelius Turner." Doc responded.

"Perhaps we should make a list of people in town who are," Moody suggested.

"You know kid, you will make an excellent inspector one day," said Raven.

"Bite your tongue. My son is going to be a doctor," challenged Doc.

"Maybe he wants to be a scientist?" Abbie chimed in.

"Don't be silly." Laurel crossed the room to embrace Moody in her arms.

Moody froze and his ears turned red.

Laurel didn't think that she'd embarrassed the boy. "He's perfect the way he is."

Raven watched the family with a covetous gaze, as he ignored the pulling sensation. He hadn't imagined a family until recently. Despite her protests, Abbie Phelan gave him hope.

CHAPTER FIFTEEN

bbie was happy. She was gathered around the table with her family and friends. She wanted to drink in the moment with those she loved.

A large turkey was being prepared as was the tradition in America – and Papa was all about tradition. Libby had done the cooking and Omar would be serving as George was feeling a bit under the weather.

Papa sat on one end of the table and Cameron Jones on the other. Abbie supposed they could each argue they were at the head and the other at the foot.

Abigail sat next to Papa and Raven next to her. Across from her sat Laurel and her husband Ben. Moody sat next to Doctor Gunn and across from Malcolm Jones.

Vasili and Emma were invited as well but decided to stay in the caravan as Molly was still uncomfortable around people. Abbie didn't blame her one bit.

Conversation flowed well over the table. She listened to Moody try and coax Cameron into a conversation about bear shifters.

"Young'un' I didn't come here to be interrogated. I came here to eat. Phelan, are you going to feed me, or do I need to go nap?"

"Didn't you get up from a nap before coming here?" Papa volleyed right back.

"Humph." Cameron Jones settled back down in his chair.

Just as Abbie hoped Mr. Jones might voice his opinion again, Omar

118

arrived with the turkey to complete the already-dressed table of wild rice imported from southern Canada.

Libby brought out juniper berry sauce along with roasted ptarmigan and potatoes.

The plates had all been served and Cameron Jones was about to eat when Vasili came running in from the kitchen. "Doctor Gunn, you need to come quick!"

Doctor Gunn stood, dropping his napkin on his chair. "What's wrong?"

"It's Emma - she's very sick and I'm worried."

"I'll come right away. Let me grab my bag from the coach." Doctor Gunn spoke as he crossed the room towards the front entry.

"I'll come with you." Laurel followed him.

Papa and Mr. Jones started to rise but Laurel stopped them. "Please enjoy your dinner. We'll be back as soon as we are able."

Vasili followed them out and Moody trailed behind.

"Papa, why don't we finish our meal and I can bring some food down to them," Abbie suggested.

"That is an excellent idea, Poppet."

The meal was eaten in silence and not even the prospect of apple pie with heavy whipped cream brought joy to the table.

Once finished, Libby and Omar boxed up the food in brass containers similar to her father's pattern mess he'd used when he was in the service. The containers clipped together top to bottom and were stacked ten high and the six stacks were clipped to Trumbo's basket. Raven, Malcolm, and Abigail decided to deliver the meals while Papa and Mr. Jones stayed behind to start notifying Alchemia's residents.

* * *

RAVEN'S NECK hair stood on end as they made their way through the cave.

"Do you smell it?" Malcolm reached into his pocket and withdrew a handkerchief and covered his nose.

Raven was about to ask 'What?' when his nose was assaulted with sickness. He hadn't smelled anything like this since the war.

"Oh, dear Lord." Abbie also stopped in her tracks. She placed her hands on her things and inhaled deep breaths.

Raven placed his hand on her back to let her know he was there. "Are you alright?"

"Just a bit of nausea." She waved him off as she placed her own foulard over her mouth.

Trumbo trotted forward, oblivious to his companions' struggles. The brass pachyderm spotted Moody and was now on a mission to the boy djinn.

Malcolm tied the kerchief behind his ears and stuffed his hands into a pair of woolen gloves.

Abbie seemed to have gathered her strength and stood straight. She turned back to the young Jones. "Are you alright, Malcolm?"

"I'll be fine." His voice was muffled behind the cloth.

Moody approached them from behind. "You should return to the house." He shooed at them with his hands.

"What's wrong?" Raven asked.

"It's some sort of contagion. Laurel, Ben, and I have all been exposed."

"Do we need to seal the entrance to the Phelan Conservatory?" Malcolm asked.

"That would be recommended."

"I'll head back and inform our parents." Malcolm retreated back down the tunnel.

"You should go with him." Moody began pushing on them.

"We are likely already exposed and you may need my help." Abbie walked past Moody towards Emma's caravan.

"How many are sick?" He wondered if the contagion was isolated or if they were looking at an epidemic.

"Nearly everyone," Moody answered.

Raven marched beside Moody until they arrived at Emma's caravan.

The door was open, but Abbie stood blocking the entrance. "Moody, can you find out if Drake Vermillion has any leeches? I need to get samples from everyone who is sick to see what we are dealing with. And, can you let Doctor Gunn know I'm gathering blood samples? And Moody,"

The boy paused.

"If you can get me a list of who is sick we could narrow down our scope." Abbie pulled her papers against her chest.

Moody plowed towards the door, nearly knocking over Raven.

"Leeches?" Raven didn't move to enter the caravan.

"Mechanical leeches. The doctor before Sophia used them, but Emma didn't allow use of them, so we outfitted the bloodsuckers for taking blood samples rather than leeching. I figure if there were any here, the resident vampire might have some." Her worried expression remained focused on Emma.

"Where are Laurel and Doc?"

"Doctor Gunn is looking in on other patients. I assume Laurel is with him." Raven stepped further into the caravan.

Emma was laid out on the bed and no one else was present.

"Where's Molly?"

"After Emma collapsed Vasili carried Molly to his caravan."

"Is Molly sick?"

"I have no idea."

"I'll track them down." Raven mulled over whether Molly had something to do with this disease spreading about the camp.

Abbie finally looked up to give him a half-hearted smile. "I'll be here."

Raven went about tracking down Molly using Vasili's scent. He tracked the smell deeper back to the fork in the cave with one path leading to the conservatory. There was a corral up in the other path on one side of the cave. Various brass animals were penned seemingly in stasis. He followed the fence line down into the tunnel until he came to an encampment.

A small caravan resembling a raindrop blocked him. There seemed hardly enough room to lie down on the feather bed inside.

Raven progressed to the back of the caravan to find Vasili shoeing a brass mule and Molly in a catatonic state on a bench beside him. "Why aren't you helping in the camp?"

"To do what? I'm no doctor. 'Sides I'm takin' care of Molly." He dropped the mule's foot.

"What's wrong with her?" Raven found her entire nature unsettling.

"Nothin' she's healthy as this brass mule here." The gypsy patted the equine's hindquarters as if the damn thing was real.

"Like brass animals do you?"

"They suit me fine. Don't have to feed 'em or worry about if they get sick?" He shrugged his hulking shoulders.

"Is that why you abandoned Emma for Molly - since she's mostly parts now?" Raven pressed him for a response.

Vasili rose swiftly, Raven didn't have time to react before the man had him about the collar and was shoving him up against the corral.

"I didn't abandon her. I wouldn't." A grief-stricken glower spread over Vasili's features before he gave a choked laugh. "Emma asked me to watch over Molly."

"Why?" Raven shook free of his grasp.

Vasili went to sit by Molly, draping an arm around her smaller shoulders. "To protect her. As you can see she's na exactly aware of her surroundings."

"Let me help you. Tell me when Molly arrived. Perhaps her story will help us now."

"She arrived sometime during the fight. Molly was placed outside Emma's caravan, much in the state you see her in now."

"The implants and the arm are new?"

"As much as I can tell." He looked away from Raven and into the small fire burning bright in the dark cave.

"What? Tell me. Whatever you know could be important."

Vasili lifted Molly's mechanical arm, "Emma suspected this might be Cornelius Turner's prosthetic."

Raven looked closely. While the hand was a delicate framework of wire and metal resembling a woman's smaller digits, as his gaze traveled upwards a cage encircled Molly's own bicep and appeared bulkier giving the apparatus the appearance it was made for a man.

"You don't have a mechanical leech do you?" he asked.

"I might." Vasili rose to go to a workbench tucked behind the bed of the raindrop vehicle. He rummaged through various parts and pulled out half a leech. "I'm still working on this one. What do you want a leech for?"

"I'd like a sample of Molly's blood. Abbie is collecting all the patients' blood."

"I told ye, Molly ain't sick." Vasili placed one hand on his hip while the other waved the half-leech.

Raven took a deep breath. "I know, but I think she's the reason the rest of the clan is ill."

As if reason suddenly dawned, Vasili gave a curt nod and quickly finished the leech.

Raven made his way back towards Abbie. A strong awareness of hope that she and Doc would find a cure for this epidemic.

* * *

ABBIE CONTINUED RUNNING a wet cloth over Emma wondering why she'd been left alone. Were most of the clan sick? She looked outside to find Trumbo patiently waiting. The food is still on his back. She laid the cloth over Emma's forehead and walked with purpose outside.

She spotted a younger girl about seventeen whom she recognized, "Colleen!"

Colleen looked up from the fire she'd been tending. "Yes, ma'am?"

She gestured for Trumbo to follow her, and his clinking sounded like little bells cutting a path of joy through this bleakness. "Would you be able to help me, or rather Trumbo?"

"I don't understand, Miss Phelan."

"We brought food down to share with Vasili and Flannigan's, but Molly and Vasili are missing and Emma is in no condition to eat. Would you like to try some?"

"Cook made it, did she? What is for dessert?" Colleen grinned as she headed for Trumbo.

"Apple pie. Actually, Libby, Laurel's maid, insisted on cooking."

Colleen stopped in her tracks.

"I assure you that pie is nearly as good as Cook's," Abbie assured her.

"Perhaps those who aren't sick could partake outside Emma's house." Colleen nodded to the long table set up with benches on either side by the caravan.

Abbie's stomach growled at the moment.

"And you could join us." Colleen winked.

The two ladies went about setting up the long table with the tins Abbie had brought as well as the stew Colleen had been tending. Others came and assembled their bounty on the table. Soon there was a hodgepodge of food including soda bread, ptarmigan, boiled beets, goulash, pickled halibut, salmon with roasted pine nuts, frozen cream with blueberry sauce, and there was even a pumpkin. So much food and so few people prompted Abbie to ask "How many are sick?"

"Nearly everyone. Only the humans among us remain healthy. This sickness is most strange." commented Olaf who was digging into the jar of pickled halibut.

The Gunn's approached the table. Their sullen faces and slow pace contrasted with the life abounding at the table.

Abbie went to greet them. "How is everything?"

"This disease has run rampant through this camp, we need to quarantine the area," Doc notified her.

"Those people aren't sick?" Laurel nodded towards the table of revelers.

"They're human," Abbie stated.

"Truly? You wouldn't have samples of their blood would you?" Doc asked.

"I have them back at the lab. They were part of our initial inquiry before this sickness broke out. Were you able to get samples from the sick?" she asked.

"Moody is finishing the task," Laurel confirmed.

They walked over to the table to join the other gypsies when Raven joined them.

"Did you find Molly?" Abbie asked.

"Yes, Emma asked Vasili to watch over her. I was able to get a sample of her blood." He held up a half-leech with a tube attached to it.

"Excellent! I'm beginning to suspect that perhaps she might be the clue to all this." Doc seated himself next to Olaf and began opening tins.

"I think you are correct. Emma and Vasili also concluded the arm attached to Molly belonged to Cornelius Turner. The arm had been modified, but it was not hers," Raven clarified.

"In what way?" Doc asked.

"Well first let me ask you, Abbie, was Mr. Turner's mechanical arm partial or complete?" Raven asked.

She retook her seat next to Colleen and answered in earnest. "It was a full arm, connecting at the socket."

"Molly's new arm is a cage from elbow to shoulder. Her hand and forearm appear to have been crafted for her, but I suspect the cage used to hold a piston, to assist a man in the mines," Raven seated himself next to her.

"This means we can place Sophia at the scene of Mr. Turner's murder." Laurel grabbed a tin from her husband before sitting on the bench next to him.

Abbie's hope rose that the whispers about her would cease and the Consortium would have no reason to back her father into a corner. Warring with hope was a desire to escape the sadness. Her good name was too high a price if keeping it pristine meant those she loved fell sick.

"Not necessarily," Doc interjected, passing Laurel another tin.

"It simply means she may have had possession of the arm, but even that is not proven yet." Raven accepted the turkey from Laurel.

"Darn. I was rather hoping to be at the end of this murder thing." Abbie's stomach rolled and the air seemed sour as she inhaled, as she realized she was no closer to clearing her name.

Her expression must have said as much as Laurel reached across the table to pet her hand. "Don't worry, Abbie, if anyone can figure out what happened Raven and Moody will."

Abbie nodded with a lightness in her chest and a sense of calm.

As they were enjoying their meal with the gypsies Moody made his way up to the table. "Did you save any food for me?"

Laurel patted the spot next to her on the bench. "Of course, I wouldn't let my son starve."

"Did you collect all the samples?" Doc asked.

"Yes." Moody reached for the tins. "They are back at the last caravan."

"I can send Trumbo with you to collect them."

Trumbo stomped his feet at the prospect of going with Moody. Her pet seemed to be very fond of the djinn.

They finished their meal and headed back toward the cave's entrance.

Vasili had given them a cart with blankets and two Gypsy Vanner Brass Steeds. The ride back to the house was cold, but Raven kept her warm as she pressed her side against him on the bench. Moody managed a small fire in a copper bowl atop Trumbo in the back, keeping his parents warm.

They were greeted by her father's sunken face at the door. "George is dead."

CHAPTER SIXTEEN

The Phelans turned their conservatory into a makeshift hospital. The Consortium provided cots which were lined along the pavers. Each disconcerting cough bounced against the glass windows before echoing down the tunnels to reach cringing ears.

The next few weeks were a blur as miners for both the Consortium and the Free Mining Company were felled by the ravaging illness.

Numerous people had died that the dead presently outnumbered the sick. And the sick outnumbered their caretakers.

Even the Cameron men had fallen ill and remained in their house.

Doc and Abbie concurred that Molly must be patient zero as she seemed unaffected.

Doc and Moody made daily rounds along with everyone. They were unwilling to risk Laurel's health once they discovered the high iron contributed to the victims' weakened immune systems.

Doc was worn down each evening, as evidenced by his Hunefeld levels reaching as high as twenty-five. Once he hibernated and turned to stone each evening his levels would once again drop back to zero.

Moody remained unaffected.

Too much time had passed without answers and Raven decided to question Sophia Pembrooke. He wasn't sure he would get anywhere, but he would feel better having tried.

The Phelan mansion had been sealed off from the Conservatory. He left through the north tunnel to reach town. Though the temperature was brisk, he remained unaffected by the weather. This illness chilled his blood more than the cold outside.

As he approached her office there was a loud noise from within the building. The boards skipped beneath his boots.

He withdrew his colt and cocked it.

Despite the closed sign, he opened the unlocked door.

He heard a man's voice shout. "No! Dead!"

Tapping on the floor he recognized Sophia's annoyed voice "I'm well aware. We need to move him. YOU need to move him. I'm not strong enough."

Raven led with his gun past the desk upfront, past her office and lab, inching his way towards the room with all the locks at the end of the hall. He would finally find what Sophia Pembrooke thought required a locked door.

"Sick and Die. Not move." The man's voice grew louder.

"You will not get sick and die. Did Molly make you sick?" Sophia cajoled.

Raven stopped just before entering the room.

Molly had been in Archangel this whole time.

Raven could almost kiss Sophia for her blunder. He could charge her with abduction.

Raven wasn't sure what he expected to find when he crossed the room's threshold but it wasn't what was left of the man in front of him. "Lord Pembrooke?"

Lord Emory Pembrooke turned to face him. He had a faraway stare and his lips were compressed. His features were void of any emotion. Pembrooke seemed as if he wasn't truly present.

"He's not actually Lord Pembrooke anymore. He's simply Emory with an emphasis on simply." Sophia responded.

"What did you do to him?" Raven asked.

"I believe the procedure is referred to as a lobotomy. However, I made some modifications."

Raven assessed Emory's body modifications, including new hands, legs, and a skull plate.

"Friend?" Emory asked.

"No." Sophia smiled, "Not friend."

Emory charged Raven, closing the distance rapidly.

Raven fired on instinct aiming for Lord Pembrooke's chest. He fired all five rounds in the cylinder.

Emory slowed falling forward and dropped in the doorway. He blocked Sophia's only exit.

"Damn it, Emory." She placed her hands on her hips.

"Sophia Pembrooke, by the power of the Free Miner Company, in conjunction with the Territory of Archangel, I'm taking you into custody for murder."

"Lewis died from this god-forsaken epidemic." She kicked Lewis emphasizing his demise.

"Not Lewis, Cornelius Turner."

"You can't prove anything, least of all murder." She crossed her hands over her chest.

"Not yet, but I'm guessing once Emory's modified hands are examined, we'll be able to place him at the crime scene."

"That only proves Emory murdered Mr. Turner."

"True, but I can hold you on suspicion of tampering with Consortium property. Or, was Molly's arm, not your handiwork? The engineering was rather high grade, perhaps someone more intelligent modified Mr. Turner's arm?"

"Are you so inept that you can't recognize quality work? It's mine. No one else could have positioned the syringe in the finger or…." She stopped before any further incriminations sprung forth.

"As I suspected." Raven stepped over Emory and Lewis. He quickly grasped Sophia's wrists pulling them behind her back.

She pulled forward and tried to step on his foot and struggled to break free of his hold.

"I'm done playing with you." Raven yanked her ramrod straight and bared his teeth.

"The devils take you, Inspector," she hissed before relinquishing her fight.

"I'm sure he will, in good time."

They made the short walk from her office to his jail; Raven didn't bother to slow his pace.

Raven finally settled Sophia within a cell and secured the lock when the front door swung open. "Moody."

"Laurel has fallen." Moody's eyes narrowed and hardened at the sight of Sophia. His mouth wrenched in an unpleasant twist as he advanced towards her.

Raven rested a hand on the boy's shoulder. "No, Scamp. We'll leave her to the authorities."

Moody's eyes glowed red. "If my mum dies, the law will not have their chance at you."

Raven ushered Moody away from the cell towards the front door.

"Go ahead, Inspector, you'll be back soon enough for answers." Sophia's contemptuous tone sparked his anger.

"Who knows? I may grant you a wish, Scamp." Raven promised in parting.

* * *

SOPHIA SAT in her cell staring at the bars. How dare they lock her up like some common criminal!

She stared at what remained of a turkey dinner the young lawman had given her. She'd taken a few bites. The food tasted wonderful. Though she was famished, she paused. She waited for about an hour before eating the remainder of her food. Her captors were going to play fair since it didn't appear she was poisoned.

Stuffed, her corset bit into her ribs. They had assigned a local boy, Logan Black, one of Constable Belle's lackeys, to watch her in Raven's little jail. She was stunned to learn that Constable Belle had succumbed to her Fae flu.

Logan snoozed quietly in his chair, his own belly stuffed.

The door opened but the boy did not wake.

Her mouth fell open when she saw a face from Constantinople. "Seamus O'Grady, is it?"

"Ye are correct, Lassie. 'Tis glad I am ye remember me."

"What are you doing here?"

"Oh, I be here to ensure your silence."

The boy still didn't rise. Perhaps he had been drugged.

"What did you do to him?"

"Oh, he be sleeping soundly. There be no reason to wake him until we've concluded our business."

"What business is that?" Her limbs began to tingle.

"Your creation of an epidemic disease among the good people of Archangel." he accused her.

"They aren't even people."

"They are my people."

"What are you?"

"Why Mrs. Pembrooke, have you never seen a Leprechaun?"

"Shouldn't you be shorter?"

"That is simply a myth. Nor do we ride rainbows. We are, however, managers of gold for the queen."

"Victoria?"

The man laughed a hollow sound. "Such small minds you humans have." He shook his head. "Enough about me and mine. Let us get down to brass tax. Why have you created a disease to wipe out my race?"

"You know my father was taken in the middle of the night by the Czar himself."

"The Royal families are only loosely tied with us. This is no reason." He waved his hand dismissively.

"No one would help him, not human, not Fae, what do I care if you and your kind are gone from this earth."

"Your father aligned himself against the Fae, he aligned himself with the Czar and the Royals' continued assault on our kind despite their Fae blood."

"What on earth are you talking about?"

"You think you are the first to come up with a scheme to wipe us out. Since the time of Arthur, when Merlin and Morgan divided the realms, Fae and humans have fought wars, disease, and each other.

"Rodent shifters helped create the Plague. We've funded your wars and even negotiated a few treaties. In the hundreds of years I've been serving Queen Morgan, we've never had such a mess as you lot from Constantinople. Breaking Treaties, fleeing to neutral territory, and now you've created a bloody disease to ravage us."

"I don't see the problem," Sophia spoke with bravado.

"No, you wouldn't, what could I expect from a Faeling," O'Grady sneered.

"I'm not one of you." She rose from her bench. "I've checked and double-checked, and I would never create a disease that might harm me."

"A madwoman." The leprechaun pulled a syringe from his pocket tapping the bubbles out.

"What is that?" Sophia backed up until the cold brick touched her shoulder blades.

"This?" He held up the syringe. "This is how you are eliminated." His voice sent cold waves rippling along her spine.

An unknown force pulled her up against the bars, stretching her arm against them. He snaked his hand between the metal barriers and inserted the needle in a vein along her hand.

The golden-red liquid burned.

"What is it?" Sophia gasped. She cradled her arm, rubbing the skin that prickled like needles. Her skin acquired a bluish hue and her veins began to rise with a golden hue.

"Oh, the potion be a lot of Fae blood, from the queen herself, you know. I suspect with your own concoction airborne, you should be dead within a few hours."

"They'll know what you did. You won't get away with it. Abigail Phelan will run tests." She could feel her muscles tense as she searched out the small cot.

"Now with all the blood you've drawn and samples you've created, why would they suspect that little poke I gave ye?"

"But I'm not Fae? They know that."

"Aye, that be true, which is the reason the queen's blood is coursing through your veins right now. Did you know that sixty percent of the human population has Fae blood and they don't even know it? Likely why your friend Lewis died along with a handful of miners."

Sophia's vocal cords tightened. The potion rendered it difficult to swallow let alone speak.

"I actually informed Lewis of this fact, and he was kind enough to leave the statistic in his notes which I'm sure Inspector Raven will find." He stared at her. "Why don't you lie down? Seems your disease and the royal Fae blood are tearing through you faster than I anticipated."

Logan made a noise in the corner.

O'Grady's eyes darted towards him, and he pulled a pistol from his chartreuse coat and waved the weapon towards the awakening Logan, "Well lassie, his awakening be my cue to leave."

He backed towards the entrance.

Sophia watched helplessly as the door clicked in the silence of the room. *Done in by a damn leprechaun!*

She watched as Logan took a long exhausted sigh and stood. He made his way over to a wash bowl and splashed water on his face. Grabbing a nearby cloth he dried away the water.

Look over here, you imbecile!

Logan dropped the cloth haphazardly on the table before sauntering over to her cell.

"Doctor Pembrooke!" Finally, he seemed to have come fully awake. "Are you alright?"

Sophia mutely shook her head.

Logan fumbled for the key to unlock the door, but his rescue was in vain.

Sophia's eyes were heavy. Each breath was like inhaling sand rather than air. Her muscles twitched and she shook uncontrollably. She took one last labored breath before closing her eyes.

CHAPTER SEVENTEEN

Raven gathered his coat and Stetson from Omar when the front door of the Phelan foyer swung open, striking the wall with a thud.

"Sophia Pembrooke is dead!"

Raven stared at Deputy Logan Black stunned. "What did you say?"

"She just died in her cell." Logan's voice was still near to shouting.

"What happened?"

Raven was stunned Logan's lanky animated arms didn't topple his cowboy hat off his wavy brown hair. His facial expressions were exaggerated causing his brown eyes to crinkle at the corners and then expand, it was a miracle they stayed in his skull. The whole descriptive ordeal of Sophia's death was dizzying.

Raven wondered if the young man would stop and breathe if his hands were tied behind his back.

"Did you bring her?" he asked after the tirade was complete.

"No! I'm not touching her."

He was afraid to ask. "How do you know she's dead?"

"I poked her with a shovel." Logan stood proud as a peacock - hands on his hips.

Raven rolled his eyes. "A classic deduction method." He rubbed the bridge of his nose. "Did you remember to lock the cell back up?"

"Yes, sir." He nodded with enthusiasm.

"Good. Why don't you go back to the jail and I'll send Moody to collect Sophia Pembrooke."

"Yes, sir." Logan saluted him and then exited the very door he'd slammed open moments before.

Raven didn't look forward to sharing this news with Abbie or Doc as he stepped along the path that led to the back entrance of the conservatory. He himself wasn't sure if Sophia's demise was good or bad. He didn't like the woman, but it was as if she had escaped justice.

Raven hadn't yet had a conversation with Abbie about their future since the deadly outbreak. Perhaps now wasn't the best time, but he wasn't certain any time would be ideal. He navigated through the barren trees and snow, unhindered by the cold this December day. The snow around the conservatory looked as if it had been pulled away from the glass. Once he opened the door, he was hit with the warmer air. The temperature wasn't overly warm this time of year in the building, but compared to outside it was damn near-tropical. He stomped his feet, shedding the snow. This is where he'd first seen his Abbie, sorting birds the night he'd arrived. He'd wondered where she had disappeared. Now he knew her and this conservatory intimately and strode a few meters to her.

Abbie's lab spilled out into the conservatory with files on carts, the archway entrance lined with racks of test tubes. On the soapstone counter were additional samples with clipboards and more files. Pages of her distinctive illegible notes consumed any remaining clear space.

When he arrived she seemed engrossed, peering into a microscope, not hearing him enter into her realm. With fascination he watched her; Pencil between her teeth, she removed it, and scribbled some notes on a nearby pad, before repeating the process again.

Raven took a breath, marveling at her beauty among the chaos.

This past week they'd fallen into a routine. He would find her collapsed from exhaustion in her lab and return her to her bedroom. He slept next to her, guarding her and listening to her heart and lungs for any sign of illness.

Every morning he woke up alone while she was off saving the world.

"I'm such an idiot." Despite Abbie's wide-eyed wonder, she seemed exhausted.

"I don't think so," he said.

She looked up. A widening smile etched her features. "You don't even know what I've found."

"I'm sure your discovery is brilliant." He closed the short distance between them. The sudden urge to touch her was his greatest wish. He held his arms out to her.

She allowed him to enfold her in his embrace. "I think you are biased."

"In the very best way. I assure you." She felt right in his arms. He leaned in, breathing in her scent.

"What are you doing here?"

"I'm afraid I have bad news." Might as well delay the inevitable a little longer. "You first. What did you find?"

"It's you. You are the key."

He wondered idly about her well-being. "I'm afraid I'm not following you. Did you get enough sleep last night?"

"Well, not you specifically. Vasili too."

The hairs on the back of Raven's neck rose. "You might want to clarify, Abbie."

"Werewolves hold the cure to this disease."

"We do?" He asked half in hope and the other in fear.

"I didn't catch the discovery right away because shifters are immune to iron. The carrier is iron, but like any virus, it mutates. Now the virus attacks Fae and shifters, but at some point, the disease will ravage the human population.

"Perhaps the virus already has," he whispered.

"What do you mean?" her eyes narrowed on him.

He didn't want to wreck her moment of discovery, but what choice did he have? "Sophia Pembrooke is dead."

"Oh no." She took a step back clutching the soapstone counter. She seemed to sway and her face turned ashen.

He heard her heart speed up and her breath increase. He needed to stop her from derailing. "So what makes werewolves so special?"

She steadied, but her tone was subdued. "Any were-animal would be immune. The Plague mutation turned shifters into werewolves, werebears or werecats and their cell structure won't support the virus or any of its subsequent mutations. Any person bitten, marked or turned would not get sick."

"Like you."

"Like me. Wolves seem generally more resilient on the shifter side. Their immunity might have something to do with the combination."

"Do you have wolf-shifters in Alchemia?"

"According to my mother's logs, the Black brothers are wolves."

"Logan Black?"

"Yep and Liam."

"That explains the puppiness of him," he muttered.

"I will let Doctor Gunn know what I've found. He may know better than I the best way to synthesize the antiserum treatment." An expression of satisfaction returned to her blue eyes.

* * *

"DOCTOR GUNN, I believe I've discovered how to cure Laurel." Abbie rushed into the bedroom before coming to a dead halt. Raven pressed into her back as he'd been right behind.

In the enjoyment of her discovery, she'd nearly forgotten her friend's beleaguered state. She walked over to the bed and stared down at Laurel sleeping. Her husband Ben holding her hand and Moody stood behind Ben as if guarding his parents.

Moody was the only one to acknowledge her with a nod.

Laurel was quiet and still.

Lost in his wife, Doctor Gunn kneeled by Laurel's bedside gazing intently as if he might will her to rise and be whole again.

Moody kneeled next to Doctor Gunn and grasped him by the shoulders. "Father."

The gesture broke the spell.

Doctor Gunn looked up and whispered a soft, barely audible, "What?"

"Abbie found something." Moody's hand remained on Laurel as he stared into Doctor Gunn's ragged and worn face.

"A cure?" Doctor Gunn was thinner and there were dark circles under his eyes.

"I hope so," she broached the subject and him. "I need your help." She reached out and grasped his shoulder. "I'm not sure how to create the vaccine."

"Laurel," Ben Gunn turned away from her, shrugging free of her.

"I will watch over her," Moody volunteered.

"This vaccine could save her life," Abbie said with more force than she intended.

"Come on, Doc! Laurel would want you to fight this by any means necessary, not watch her die. She's likely to take my head when she looks at you." Raven broke through the melancholy permeating the air of the room.

"You'd have to get in line. She'd have a go at me first." Doctor Ben let out a hollow laugh.

"You are the only one who can help Miss Phelan. You must go." Moody said in all seriousness.

Doctor Gunn stood, dusted himself off and walked like a man going to the gallows.

They walked in silence back to the conservatory.

Before they reached the lab, Doctor Gunn stopped and grabbed a cup of tea at a station set up along the pathway. There were biscuits and other beverages constantly being stocked so the volunteers could continue monitoring patients. "What do you need from me?"

Abbie led the men to an alcove of the conservatory near the rubber palms which provided a modicum of privacy. "It would seem the initial carrier was iron and that the were-creatures are immune to the disease."

"Immune, you say?" Doctor Gunn's eyes suddenly held a small glow and his stature seemed a bit taller than she'd seen him in days.

"I'm not sure if the vaccine will work on all those affected. I wanted to ask a few clarifying questions."

"Shoot." Doctor Gunn sat down on a bench with his eyebrows arched in a scrutinizing stare.

"So the reason I think this might be the cure is that I've been bitten by Raven. Unlike you, I can't restore myself. I'm as much Fae as Emma and I've been exposed to this virus as long as you, yet I show no signs of illness."

"Hmm, mmm." Doctor Gunn nodded, setting his cup down on the bench, and steepled his hands against his chin.

"However, I'm not sure if it's the were-blood, or if any immune Fae creature would work, or even if we have to mix and match. For instance, Raven's blood might immunize me, but maybe not Laurel."

"Or Moody's blood could cure Laurel." He stood and strode down the cobble path towards her lab.

Abbie picked up her skirts to follow at his rapid pace.

"Or maybe that vampire, Drake!" Raven called from behind her.

Once they reached the lab, some of the steam came out of Doctor Gunn. "How do you know where anything is?"

Abbie's nerves ruffled at his comment. "I have a system."

Doctor Gunn turned on her. "Chaos is not a system."

Raven stepped between them. He grasped her shoulders, fixed his gaze on her, and extended a compassionate smile. "Abbie, could we place Doc in your aviary lab?"

Abbie's heart clenched. This man understood her like no other. He may not be a scientific mind, but he was her soul mate. "Yes. Those counters are all clear and we can bring over anything, samples, files, etc. that Doctor Gunn needs."

Doctor Gunn peeked around Raven. "Fine. I want the files of those not sick and you can give me a status on their lineage. I also want blood samples of Moody, Raven, Vasili, and this vampire."

"And Sophia Pembrooke's body?" Abbie squeaked.

At Doctor Gunn's mutinous gaze, Raven relayed the events of Sophia Pembrooke's demise.

"Fine." Doc waved his hand dismissively. "Send her corpse to me and I'll take a look."

Raven smirked, "Well Doc, get going and I'll be along with whatever you need."

Doctor Gunn marched out the doorway down the path likely towards the aviary.

"Do you need help finding anything?" Raven wrapped his arms around her waist pulling her close.

She nodded to the files by the door. "Those are the files of the non-sick, blood vials of Moody, Vasili and you."

"The Vampire?" he nuzzled her neck.

She shook her head. "I don't have his blood."

He pulled back, "But you do have a system?"

"Of course. My office just looks like a mess to everyone else."

"I love you, Abigail Phelan." He smiled before he leaned in and kissed her.

Doc was finally settled in the aviary lab after a day. Abbie and Raven found him nestled in a corner desk with his files, neatly stacked. There were blood samples and vials in orderly rows on the lab counters and the instruments were pushed to the back unless in use.

Raven sent Abbie a side-glance. If she was unsettled by the anti-chaos, she gave no indication. "What do you need, Doc?"

"I need you to take this vaccine to the shifters." Doc nodded to the purplish colored vials on the counter and checked his notes. "The Black and the Cameron families. If they give you names of other shifters, come back for more."

"What is it?" Abbie lifted the vial towards the light filtering in from the window.

"Human flu virus, werewolf blood, and gold."

"Gold?" Raven asked bemused.

"Yes, the precious metal seems to help expedite the reaction, and I feel quick response and data analysis is what we need to cure Laurel."

"What if your experimental vaccine kills them?" The idea that Doc's solution could harm his fellow shifters made Raven queasy.

"I don't anticipate death to be a reaction. When was the last time you had a cold, Raven?"

"Maybe when I was a child, but not since I've reached adulthood."

"I imagine your resistance is due to your shifter genes. That's why we are testing this vaccine on the other shifters; I don't anticipate they will have a reaction other than maybe a cold if that. Because Shifters don't have Were-Antibodies I suspect they will have some reaction, but nothing severe. Start with the Black family and move onto the Cameron clan."

"Alright," Abbie nodded and turned back to Raven. "Let's go!"

Raven followed Abbie the whirlwind as she navigated efficiently towards her own lab grabbing her short-trimmed fur jacket off the rack and marching out to her waiting steam carriage. They rode in silence, the first few miles, but Raven became curious. "Have you known either of these shifter clans to fall ill?"

"Yes. Malcolm got a cold so bad once he was laid up for a week."

"How often did you get sick?" He was still worried about her.

"Nothing serious. I've been laid up for a day or two, but recovered quickly. Of course I didn't know the things I know now." She retreated back into the carriage seat.

Raven let her have her moment of solitude.

When they reached the Black family home, Abbie knocked on the door. A man with a square jaw, brown eyes and dark hair short yet still long enough to fall over his brow answered the door. He sniffed the air and his eyes cut towards Raven.

"You're a were-creature." He snarled at Raven. He didn't even acknowledge Abbie.

"Yes. We're here on behalf of Doctor Benjamin Gunn, who's been assisting Miss Abigail Phelan with this epidemic." Raven said, returning to the matter-at-hand.

"Phelan," the man he believed was Mr. Black nodded towards Abbie.

"Black," Abbie shoved past Raven.

"You can't just come barging in here Phelan, we have rights. And this tainted blood is not welcome." Black blocked her entry. The man was wise enough to not place hands on her.

Abbie gasped. "What do you mean tainted?"

"He's a were. They have tainted blood-lines."

"Of all the stupid things, I've ever heard. It's called adaptation."

Raven exhaled. Abbie considered his were-blood a normal adaptation. Her acceptance continued to be a relief.

"I'm trying to help you, you dumb-witted oaf." Abbie pushed on Black's shoulders and the strong man shuffled backward.

"I take it you know each other?" Raven asked as he followed his mate into the one-room cabin.

"We're cousins." They replied in unison.

"You have a cousin?" Raven asked, stepping back, momentarily dazed.

"On my mother's side" Abbie clarified.

"Our mothers were already distant cousins," Black added.

"Regardless, I've brought a vaccine from Doctor Gunn. I'd like to administer it to you." Abbie held up the vials.

"No," Black said.

"No." Abbie advanced on Black. "Are you crazy? This cure could save your life." She punctuated the center of his chest with her finger.

"As you can tell, Logan and I aren't sick." Black stretched out his limbs taking up space.

"Have you been exposed?" Raven asked.

"At least a dozen times or more. Who do you think hauled the sick out of Baranov's mines?"

"A traitor to his own kin." Abbie crossed her arms over her chest.

"Look Imp, just because your father has finally told you all the family secrets doesn't mean I like the man."

"What do you mean?" she asked.

"Your father is the reason our families aren't close. He forbade us to tell you what we were. And after our Pa died in the mining accident of 1861, we sure as hell couldn't live with your perfect little family."

"You could have," she insisted.

"You think Logan and Luna could've hidden what they were. They were too young to know better. I had to take that mining job to support them. You think I wanted to send Luna to the states to live?" Black's voice ended in a near howl.

"I didn't know." Abbie's lips pressed together.

"Well, now you do. We got by fine without Phelan money then and we'll do fine without your cure now." Black's eyes were hard.

"Liam, I…." Abbie reached towards the man.

"Don't Imp. The past can't be fixed." Black turned away from her.

Raven enclosed his arms around Abbie. "Abbie let us go to the Camerons."

"Gonna try your luck with some bears." Black's laugh sounded hollow. "Funny how your father aligned with them but not his own kin."

Abbie's head was down, yet Raven heard her nearly inaudible sniffle and smelled the salt of her tears. He watched as she turned toward the brass animal carriage and climbed in.

Raven shut the cabin door behind him and slammed Black up against it. "If you weren't her family, and we weren't in the middle of this epidemic, I'd call you out."

"Funny, I could say the same of you." Black threw his head back and bared his canines.

Raven stumbled. "What?"

"Your scent is running straight through her. If you don't make it right, I'll call you out regardless of the circumstances." Black was stronger and shook free of Raven's hold.

"You think I haven't tried," Raven countered. "She won't have me."

"Doesn't matter, even her own father should've taken you to task? Unless the man is blind?" Black advanced towards him.

Raven's jaw moved but no words came forth. He hadn't considered asking Edmund Phelan for his daughter's hand. He was reasonably sure Professor Phelan wouldn't force her, but at least the man would know his intentions were honorable. "I'll speak to him."

"Then I'll see you at the wedding," Black smiled.

"After that little tirade with my mate, you won't be invited."

Black huffed and Raven left.

* * *

THEY SAT in the carriage silent on the way over to the Cameron Household, which was fine with Abbie. Her core knotted and her mind reeled with confusion and shame that Liam had wrought on her. How dare he suggest her father hid her heritage from her? Hadn't Papa revealed everything when she asked? She was sure he had a good reason.

Raven stood with his hand out to let her down from the carriage.

So lost in thought Abbie missed their arrival. "Sorry."

"Are you okay?" he asked.

"Yes. Let's get on with this. I can't imagine this will be worse." She exited the carriage without accepting Raven's hand.

They approached the circle of cabins. There was a large cabin in the center, with two smaller cabins attached on either side.

"This is unusual," Raven said.

"The large cabin is Cameron's and the smaller ones are for Malcolm and Lachlan"

"Lachlan?"

"Cameron's oldest son."

"I haven't met him."

"You wouldn't have. He's gone. They mostly use the house for guests." Abbie was about to knock on the main cabin door when it creaked open.

Cameron Jones greeted them, "What do you want Abbie? Inspector?"

"Mr. Jones. How are you feeling?" Abbie noted his pale skin and the dark circles beneath his eyes.

"I'm doing better." Mr. Jones opened the door allowing them entrance. "And Malcolm?"

"Not as well, he still has a fever." Mr. Jones shuffled over to a nearby chair, grabbed the quilt off the back, and wrapped the thick material around his limbs.

"That's why I'm here. We may have found a cure." Abbie hoped this would help Malcolm through the worst of the disease.

"What's the catch?" He coughed before taking a sip of a steaming liquid on his table.

"What are you drinking, sir?" she asked.

"Tottie. You want a sip?" he raised his cup to her.

"No, thank you. May I see Malcolm?"

Cameron Jones nodded to the cabin door behind him on the right.

Abbie walked to the door and opened it slightly, peeking in.

The heat hit her first. The room was like an oven. She widened the door to let some air in.

Beads of sweat dotted Malcolm's forehead and he gleamed under the glow of the fire.

"How long has he been like this?" Abbie asked.

"The last day or so," Mr. Jones spoke right behind her. his stealth indicated even ill, shifters were still quick and silent. "He collapsed and I had a few of the miners place him in here. He hasn't moved since."

"Who is taking care of him?" Raven asked from the entrance door.

"I am. Everyone else is too sick." Mr. Jones shrugged.

"I'd like to give you both the vaccine," Abigail couldn't bear to see Malcolm this way and Mr. Jones looked as though the reaper was getting ready to guide him to the river Styx.

"I don't need it. If I die from this disease, so be it. Doubt I will though. I've lived through worse." He hobbled back to his chair, groaning as he seated himself.

"And Malcolm?" she asked.

"Give him your treatment." Mr. Jones gave her a brief nod, before leaning back and closing his eyes.

Abbie reached into her pack to grab the syringes Doctor Gunn had given her.

"Sir, you should know the vaccine has werewolf blood in it," Raven interjected from the front door.

"So?" Cameron asked.

"Some shifters would consider the blood tainted." Raven held his chin up.

Abbie was reminded of her cousin and his comment regarding tainted bloodlines.

"What do I care if he can't shift anymore?" Cameron looked as though he could care less about the purity of bloodlines. "Give him the shot."

Abbie advanced into the room, sweat gathering beneath her clothes at the intense heat.

Malcolm had a sheet tangled around his waist and covers bunched in corners of the bed. He appeared to be nude, but Abbie had no time to wonder about his state of dress and the propriety of her actions.

She lifted the syringe, tapped out any bubbles, and injected the needle into his bicep.

Malcolm turned his head and growled. His eyes never opened.

She quickly pulled the needle out.

"Raven, I'm going to need some help," she called.

Raven was immediately at her side.

"Hold him down. I don't want him to break the needle."

Raven pressed his hands down against Malcolm's shoulders.

Abbie injected him once again, emptying the vaccine into his muscle.

Raven waited a few minutes as Malcolm ceased his struggles before releasing him. Sick Malcolm was no match against Raven's health.

Abbie exited the room with Raven closing the door behind them.

"It's done then?" Cameron called from his chair.

"Yes." Abbie prayed the formula Doctor Gunn created would save her friend. "I'm sorry. He won't be able to shift again."

Cameron Jones lay his head against the back of his chair and let out a sigh. "I don't care, as long as he lives."

CHAPTER NINETEEN

The days leading towards Christmas were filled with giving each of the sick the vaccine created by Doctor Gunn. He administered it to each patient in Phelan Conservatory under his care.

On the eve of Christmas, Raven and Abbie went to town, distributing the vaccine to those who would accept it - tainted blood and all. They also collected blood samples from creatures that allowed them and ended up enjoying festivities with their patients. They arrived home later than usual and were greeted in the front entry by her father, Omar, and Libby.

Papa opened the door for them as if preparing to leave. "Oh good! I was just about to take my brass steed to search you out."

"What's happened?" Abbie asked, concerned.

"Laurel is awake," he said.

Abbie dashed up the stairs to Laurel's room.

Raven was on her heels.

She swung the door open.

Doctor Gunn, stethoscope in hand, turned and stared his mouth agape.

"Sorry," she mumbled.

"I'm glad you are here," Laurel reached her hand out.

"Are you fully recovered?" Abbie crossed the room and clasped Laurel's hand in hers before sitting down on the bed.

"Very nearly," Laurel spoke in a hoarse voice.

Abbie turned to Doctor Gunn, "Werewolf blood?"

"No, actually I used a mix of mine and Moody's blood." He said as he pressed the stethoscope to Laurel's chest. "Quiet now."

Abbie waited patiently as Doctor Gunn listened to his wife's heart and lungs. He tenderly touched Laurel's neck and looked into her eyes.

"My heart, you seem to be on the mend." Peace of mind was etched in his features as he held Laurel's hand in his. "I'd feared I'd lost you."

"I think you did for a bit." Laurel's eyes misted over.

Abbie stood and backed out of the room silently, closing the door with a click to give the couple a moment of privacy.

Raven stood outside the door. "Is Laurel alright?"

"Yes, she seems to be, according to her husband."

"Good." He descended the stairs.

She followed.

"I think it will take a bit to see Alchemia fully recovered, but we are well on our way." The significance of life regaining normalcy comforted her.

"Abbie, we need to talk." He stopped at the landing.

She sighed. "Must we?"

She wasn't ready for whatever this conversation might bring.

He gave her a probing stare. "Yes. I need to."

Abbie's stomach clenched. A sure sign she wasn't ready to hear whatever Raven had to say.

"Abbie, this is important, it's about our future."

Her head began to spin.

"I love you," Raven admitted.

"And I love you," Abbie clutched his shoulders, needing to ground herself.

"I want to make things right," he continued.

"Right, Raven I...I...I don't feel well." Abbie leaned into Raven's hard chest, letting her eyes grow heavy and the world go dark.

* * *

ABBIE FAINTED in Raven's arms.

"Doc! Doc!" Raven hollered even as he lifted her in his arms and ascended the staircase.

When he reached Laurel's room, he kicked the door with his foot.

"What the hell, Raven!" Doc stormed over, preventing Raven's entrance.

"She fainted. Something's wrong," He gripped Abbie tighter, his heart pounding against his ribs.

"Okay. Calm down, let's have a look. Lay her next to Laurel."

Laurel scooted over, making space for the next patient.

Doc placed his hands against her head. "No fever."

Raven released a sigh, closed his eyes, and nodded.

"She does feel clammy. Were you very busy today?" he asked.

"No more than usual."

"Did she eat lunch?"

"I'm not sure. I can get her some food now."

"She's not exactly in a position to eat, Raven," Laurel responded matter-of-factly.

Doc undid a few of Abbie's blouse buttons.

Raven growled.

"None of that now. I'm simply listening to her lungs, to make sure we aren't dealing with something more nefarious." Doc's tone was coolly censured.

Raven forced himself to calm down. He had to remain focused. Abbie's health was more important than his possessiveness.

Doc pressed the stethoscope to Abbie's chest. "Heart sounds good." He moved the stethoscope to her lower lungs, "Lungs are clear," and down to her abdomen. "Huh," Doc's voice dropped in volume.

"What?" Is she okay?" Raven asked.

"Yes. She's fine. She will be very hungry when she wakes up." Doc stated.

"Is her stomach growling?" Laurel smiled.

"I imagine she'll have a strong appetite." Doc winked at his wife.

"Oh." Laurel's eyes rounded.

"Raven, has Abigail been getting ill?" Doc asked.

"She got sick this morning, but she appeared healthy otherwise." Raven shrugged his shoulders.

"Just this morning?" Laurel asked. "No other mornings."

"No, I've stayed with her. She hasn't been sick other than this-- Is she? Do you mean she's ...?"

"I think the phrase you're looking for is 'with child,'" Laurel giggled.

"Laurel is correct."

"With my child." Raven leaned back against the wall, fighting the buckle of his knees.

"I would imagine so," said Doc.

"What should I do?" Raven asked.

"Make an honest woman of her," Professor Phelan's voice came from the hallway.

"I will sir. I meant to speak with you regarding my relationship with your daughter." Raven straightened facing the Professor.

"Good. Good. You have my blessing," her father replied.

"What about her health?" Raven asked Doc.

"I'm sure she is as hungry as a bear or perhaps a werewolf since she's eating for two. She should also drink more water," Doc recommended.

"So make sure she eats and drinks when she awakes," Raven spoke more to himself than the room at large.

"Yes," they all responded in unison and proceeded to laugh.

"All right. I'm not sure what's so funny." His face felt hot and his jaw clenched. "I thought her fainting was something serious."

They laughed more.

Raven had enough of their teasing. He lifted Abbie. "I'm taking Abbie to her room."

"Fine." Doc chuckled and wiped his eyes.

Raven ignored them and left to return his mate to her sanctuary.

"I'll send Libby down with some food," Laurel called after him.

* * *

ABBIE WALKED through a haze of fog.

There was Sophia Pembrooke, but wasn't she dead?

Wait. This was the night Cornelius Turner died.

Abbie uncovered the cage in Sophia's office, and the invisibirds flickered.

"These will be perfect? And how does their invisibility work?" Sophia asked.

"It's undetermined, but I've been training them to be invisible as you asked. They will not disturb your patients."

"Wonderful, and have they been vaccinated?"

"Um, no. Why?"

"Well, I don't want them to fall ill over the very people they will be watching. What if we have an epidemic?"

"I hadn't thought of that."

"Do you think it will be a problem if I vaccinate them?"

Abbie paused. She didn't want her birds to die during the vaccination process. "Would it be possible to let them catch the epidemic if one arrives and deal with vaccinations then?"

"I think your solution would work."

The door on the outside rang.

"Just a moment," Sophia spoke before exiting her office.

Abbie waited and then she heard arguing.

She walked out into the hallway.

"Cornelius!" she called him.

"Miss Phelan, what are you doing here?" he lowered his head to stare at her.

"I'm dropping off some birds for Doctor Pembrooke. How about you?"

"I'm trying to collect my paperwork from the good doctor, but she's refusing to give it. This witch has been taking blood samples from the free miners but won't tell us why." Cornelius Turner grabbed Sophia's arm.

Sophia managed to break free and raced past Abbie to her locked back room. She opened the large door quickly. "Emory! Help!"

A hulk of a man - no he was more machine than man - came out. His eyes rimmed red and he growled, like a feral beast.

"Kill them!" Doctor Pembrooke pointed at Abbie and Cornelius.

The monster lunged towards Abbie, but before the creature pounced on her, Cornelius threw Abbie behind him.

"Run Abbie! Run!" he shouted.

Abbie stood dumbfounded and watched as the animal ripped off Mr. Turner's mechanical arm.

Blood sprayed like a steam pipe, splattering across Abbie's gown.

Cornelius Turner crumpled to the floor.

Abbie turned to run but was lifted from the ground and held up by the man beast.

"Pretty," the monster said.

Suddenly he was assaulted by the invisibirds who rushed at his face, forcing him to drop Abbie. She bolted towards the door, but Sophia stopped her.

Abbie heard her birds' strangled cries and caught the tiny bodies as they flew past her vision - killed by the beast as they fought for her freedom.

"Please, stop." Tears flowed from Abbie's eyes.

The monster finished pounding the cage against the floor until the birds fell silent. The horrible creature sidled up beside Sophia. "Kill mean birds. Kill girl?"

Sophia held up a hand. "No. I have a better idea. Hold her." she shoved Abbie toward the beast and he held her firm.

"You won't get away with this!" Abbie struggled in vain. "I will report this to the authorities."

Sophia removed a pocket watch from her apron waist and swung the brass-cased timepiece back and forth in front of Abbie's face. "That is unlikely, my dear. To report anything, you would have to remember." A sinister smile passed Sophia's face.

CHAPTER TWENTY

A bbie awoke to a scone waving beneath her nose.

"You're supposed to eat. Doc said so." Raven poked her lips with the pastry.

Abbie pushed the bread away and sat up.

"How's your stomach?" Lines deepened along his brow and under his eyes.

She eyed him with suspicion. "What do you mean?"

"Doc said you fainted because you probably hadn't eaten," he said. His tone was flat, yet gentle.

"What else did he say?" What had happened while she was unconscious?

"Do you not know, Abbie?" An eager expression flickered over him.

"Yes. I know I should have eaten before we finished the last of the deliveries." Why was he being evasive?

"Do you remember getting sick this morning and saying your illness was something you ate?"

"Yes, but I'm not sure what my stomach has to do with-- Oh dear? Did I contract the sickness?" She'd been careful and sure she was immune because of Raven's bite.

"Not in the way you think."

"What are you trying to say?" Was she dying? Had she and Doctor Gunn miscalculated the effects of a werewolf bite?

"I'm trying to get you there on your own." He leaned forward as if trying to coax words from her. Infuriating man!

"Trying to get me where?" Abbie's chest tightened and her mind raced, searching for an answer.

"Remember when we had Vasili bite Emma to confirm your theory?" He sounded exasperated.

"Yeah, and the bite didn't work." She guessed with fearful clarity. "That's why I fainted, I'm not immune."

"Oh, you're immune. You just aren't getting antibodies from my bite." The beginning of a smile tipped the corners of his mouth.

"If not from you then how? You're speaking in riddles. Tell me, Raven!"

"You are getting antibodies from my child." His face split into a wide grin of satisfaction.

"What? Don't be silly, how would I get antibodies from your chi--" The truth jolted through her like Teslatricity through Trumbo's circuits. "I'm pregnant."

"Yes. Doc confirmed your condition following your fainting spell." The pride in his voice was unmistakable, and she swore she felt his swagger.

"Oh, my." She imagined the tiny life coiled within her.

"Ahem."

Abbie looked up to see her father standing in the doorway.

Raven stood, "Sir, I haven't--"

Papa waved his hand. "It's alright, my boy. We have time. I wanted to see how my girl was faring."

"I'm fine, Papa, if a bit surprised," she answered truthfully.

"Damn, I wish your mother was alive." He ran a hand through his thinning white hair.

"You and I both." She needed to speak with her father. "Raven, could you give us a moment?"

"I...ah…"

"Go along, boy," her father made a shooing motion at him.

Raven reluctantly left.

Her father sat in the vacant chair. "Well, Poppet, what is it?"

"Liam."

Her father stiffened.

"Papa, why didn't you let them tell me?"

He leaned forward in his chair. "It wasn't that I didn't want you to know, but I also knew I had to keep you safe."

"I don't understand why you wouldn't let them live here after their father was killed."

"Who said that?" he asked with a concerned expression on his face.

"Liam."

"It's not true. The Blacks were always welcome in this home. Their father, Ian, was not fond of me. He believed I had tainted your mother's line."

Abbie remembered Liam's comments about bloodlines. She also recalled Ian Black not being especially nice during her childhood.

Her father looked beyond her as if seeing the past. "If I must be honest, I think Ian Black loved your mother. They were engaged before your mother and I met."

"Truly?"

"Yes. Honestly, all we cared about was one another. We didn't anticipate the consequences of our whirlwind courtship. So, we eloped. Then I was stationed and moved from the Northeast to India."

"Papa, I had no idea."

"It wasn't something you needed to know until now."

"There was an agreement between the clans. I think Ian had to settle for Daphne's cousin. He has held a grudge ever since. I don't think he forgave me or apparently you. I am sorry for that, Poppet."

"Would it be alright if we invited Liam and Logan to Christmas dinner? To try and mend fences." She searched his face for changes.

"I'll send a messenger around." He rose to leave.

"Papa?"

"Yes?" Her father turned back towards her.

"What do you think of having a grandchild?"

"I will love you and my grandbaby regardless of their bloodline."

"And their father?"

"Do you love him?"

"I do."

"Then make an honest man of him." He winked at her as he departed.

* * *

CHRISTMAS DAY ARRIVED.

Raven asked Abbie to meet him in the Conservatory. He hadn't seen her since yesterday when she spoke to her father. His heart pounded, and his stomach fluttered like the birds in their cages. He'd never met anyone like Abigail. What if she said, no?

What if she was too normal and he was too much of a tainted freak?

Abigail liked him well enough to sleep with him. And clearly, a baby resulted from their union, but that didn't mean she'd want the father of their child.

Raven was overwhelmed and enamored with her; she had wormed her way beneath his skin and into his heart. He admitted he hadn't been careful with Abbie like he'd been with others in the past. No, he fully courted the consequences of her innocence, her body, and fates willing - her heart.

He couldn't imagine his life without her. Her bright innocence balanced out the horror that touched him. Her passion was a balm on his jaded encounters with other women.

Raven paced the cobblestones; certain he was wearing a pattern into the path. His breath hitched at the clean smell of her. Plants and orchids tinted the edge of her scent.

He lifted his head and openly studied her.

"Raven, why did you want to meet out here?" she asked, raising her voice to be heard over the birds that had suddenly seen their mistress.

"It seems appropriate to be surrounded by the things you love." By her side was Trumbo. He'd grown to like the small brass elephant. The animal reminded him more of a dog with its programmed personality, rather than the brass beasts of burden he'd seen.

The color drained from her face and her eyes widened, "You're leaving aren't you?"

"No. I'm planning to settle here."

"What's wrong?" she asked in a choked voice.

"What do you mean?"

"You're nervous. Your claws have come out." She nodded at his growing nails.

His fangs had stretched as well. "Why don't we sit?" He drifted along the cobbles to the nearest cedar bench. The conservatory was terribly humid. Why did he pick this place to propose?

She bristled, not bothering to sit. "What do you have to say?"

Trumbo nudged the back of her thighs.

He was fairly mucking his proposal up. He fingered beneath his collar wishing he had proposed nude. But no, he put on a suit. Might as well do this right. Raven got down on one knee, grasped her hand, and spoke.

"Abbie, I've never met anyone like you. You're beautiful both inside and out. My soul isn't as pure as yours. I've seen the ugly side of life. I know I don't deserve you and you could do much better than me.

"That's not true." Tears welled at the rim of her sapphire eyes threatening to drown her freckles.

"Let me finish. I hope I will be enough for you." Raven reached into his pocket and held out the ring.

"My mother's ring, but how did you..."

"When I told Laurel and Ben my plans, she insisted."

Abbie tentatively accepted the ring. She slid the treasured jewel on her finger. "It fits."

Raven stood.

Abbie threw her arms around his neck. "Thank you. This ring is the only thing I have of her." Her grip grew tight matching her voice.

"You're welcome." Raven was lost in the blue depths of her eyes and realized she hadn't said, 'Yes.'

"Is that a 'No'?"

She looked at him with an impish smile. "I'm sorry, what was your question?"

He hadn't actually asked. He was erratic and worried about what she might say; he completely forgot to ask Abigail Phelan to be his bride. "Will you marry me?"

"Of course. It's not as though fate has given me a choice."

"Because you are with my child?"

"Well, yes, but that is not the reason. You do know I love you?" She leaned into him, tilting her face towards his.

"I do recall you screaming at me." He remembered the phrase shouted during the height of her climax but did not attribute much to words spoken in the thick of passion.

"I didn't scream it," she said, blushing.

"You're right. Hollered, shouted, yelled maybe," he said before leaning down to kiss her. When he lifted his head, she held a serious note to her face.

"You never said the words back." She pulled free of his hold.

"I did before you fainted nearly dead away," he said and pushed his hands deep into his pockets to prevent pulling her back.

"My head was swimming; I don't recall much right beforehand." She seated herself on the bench.

"Abbie, if I didn't love you, I would not ask you to marry me." His voice was firm.

"Not even out of obligation?" She rested her hand on her abdomen.

"I would, but I loved you before I knew," he reasoned.

"Oh." She looked deflated but recovered just as quickly. "Actually, I have something for you as well." She reached into her apron and pulled out a small red velvet satchel.

She dumped the bag unceremoniously in her palm, before reaching in with her hand to retrieve a small object.

He seized the small stone from her, examining the craftsmanship and detail. "Abbie, I don't know what to say."

"It's a cream moonstone eye. Your patch doesn't bother me, but I recall how my makeshift one kept rubbing off during our lovemaking, and I had some special work done on this one."

He looked closer and the pupil was a black wolf and on the inner brown iris was lettering. He read out loud, "*As long as the moon rises I shall love you. Yours, Abigail.*"

"It obviously won't match your eye, but I flirted with the idea that I might enjoy looking at it." She suddenly looked down and away as if embarrassed.

He lifted her chin. "I love you, Abigail Phelan."

She stood and wound her arms back around his neck and kissed him. "How soon can we be married?"

"As soon as you wish."

"Sunday, at service."

He nodded.

"As soon as possible I wish to be Mrs. Abigail Clarke."

"So be it."

And it was.

THE END

LETTER TO MY READERS

Dear Reader,

I hope you enjoyed *Alchemists of Archangel.* Feel free to leave a review at your favorite site for other readers. I would greatly appreciate it.

I've included the first Chapter (rough draft) of Book 3 in the Archangel Revolution series, *Curse in the Caravan,* in the following pages, for your pleasure.

Feel free to follow me on social media. All my links can be found on my website, www.tinaholland.com. You can also sign up for my newsletter there. I only email regarding upcoming releases or deals that my publishers are running.

Thanks again for purchasing this book. Your patronage is appreciated.

Sincerely,

~Tina Holland

ABOUT CURSE IN THE CARAVAN

Emma Flannigan is trying to save her sister, Molly, who was left for dead in a foreign land. In order to make her sister whole, Emma needs the one thing that betrays everything she stands for. A gargoyle's heart.

Halvor is a man out of time. He's been resurrected centuries into the future and all he wants is revenge on the witch, Astrid, who cursed him. The only problem, Astrid has been dead for centuries.

When Halvor discovers the Flannigan sisters are Astrid's descendents will he take his revenge. Or will Emma who holds his heart destroy him.

CHAPTER ONE

The needle pierced Emma's skin, a sure sign her mind was elsewhere and not on her latest client's project. She sucked the blood off her index finger before making sure she hadn't damaged the white dress. Setting the material aside, she knew exactly what consumed her thoughts. Her sister, Molly. Ever since she had returned to her side, Emma knew something was not quite right with her twin.

Molly was withdrawn and silent. She had not uttered a single word since landing on the shores of Archangel. Emma only wished she'd known what that evil doctor – Sophia Pembrooke had done. She had no idea, nor did anyone else in the town. Molly Flannigan was a shell and Emma knew the only thing that would help was a gargoyle's heart and it just so happened that she knew where to find one.

She knew a gargoyle personally, but she did not intend to retrieve Dr. Benjamin Gunn's heart, not with the man married to a banshee. Besides, she had grown fond of his wife, Laurel.

Two days later she was ready. In her trunk passed down from generations, she had found her family's original grimoire. The edge of the book had years of dust and the pages were delicate, Emma had worn gloves so as not to permanently damage the tome.

Within the pages were some very old and powerful spells. Luckily, she didn't have to go very far in to find a spell that would work. *Returning the Soul.* The spell had basic ingredients and she was able to find most of what she needed, the spell called for the stone's heart, which was a bit odd. Perhaps stone heart was an ancient name for a gargoyle heart.

With this stone heart
I return my heart's desire
To reunite my family's soul
And extinguish Hel's fire
With my phoenix gone
And I'm left alone
I place this stone heart into the fire
Bring me what my heart desires
I offer this gift to Queen Morgan
Reverse the curse of the Gorgon

Nothing happened.

Emma looked over the spell to make sure she had the right ingredients. The blood of a ram - the butcher thought it an odd request, but she was able to obtain it. Elfleaf - readily available in the Phelan conservatory. Dragon Fire - hard to obtain but worth the price. And lastly the heart of a gargoyle. She was certain it was correct.

It was Samhain, and really the last time she could perform the spell while the veil was thinned. The fae owed her family a debt and it was time they paid it.

In all the years that her family had been given the gift of the phoenix- a witch who could resurrect after burning- no one had used it. Molly had died by fire so she should be resurrected by it as well.

She looked around her caravan. Despite her small surroundings the magick her family had been given kept a substantial amount of her possessions hidden. But she was indebted to the fae queen. Her entire family was. They served the fae queen to keep tabs on the Royals. When an assignment came to join the Americas, Emma had leapt at the chance, it had been her only means of escape. But even here the fae clutches reached out.

Cahir Barthiom was here already establishing a foothold for her majesty. If the fae could establish a foothold in the Archangel before the impending revolution then Morgan would have her land, a place for her people. The problem was the New World was already a land with strong spiritual beliefs.

Shifters which neither walked in the human world nor in the fae were strong here still and witches who broke from the fae and had formed their own covens were also nestled in the Americas. Even without the Americans, if Queen Morgan thought she could pry Archangel from the Romanovs without the rest of the royal families backing them she was sorely mistaken.

Perhaps the spell took some time to work like the heart had to burn to ash. Dragon fire did burn for a long time when using a magical object, such as a wand or the heart of a magical beast.

The longer the flame burned around the stone heart, the more Emma wondered if the fae had tricked her family. Fae were not known for being honest or truthful.

If this did not work she could always buy a youthful heart in the Obsidian Market, but she would have to wait a whole year before she could perform the spell again.

The gargoyle's heart had been passed down through the generations, with the spell. Maybe the heart was bad. She watched as the stone glowed with renewed life. She hadn't felt anything though. She lifted up the paper to triple-check the ingredients and incantation and suddenly the spell burst into flame.

"No!" She quickly doused the flames in a nearby bucket of water, but the parchment had been burned except for the words, 'my heart desires'.

Feeling nothing left for it she tossed the scrap into the heart now burning with a steady glow. Emma couldn't help but say a prayer afterward to give Molly the best chance of coming back.

* * *

Breaking the silence of the dark cold night, Halvor awoke from his stone slumber with a roar.

He was free.

Free to pursue those who had damned him to this mortar hell.

Where was the *volve* who had improsed him. Damn Astrid for imprisoning him, but she had wanted to impress the Saxon king with her gifts. Only she was capable of breaking the wretched curse. Well he would find her and have his revenge.

He leapt down from the merlon. He felt stronger and was surprisingly warm despite his lack of furs on this cold night. Despite the lack of moon, he could see very well. Mayhap this curse was not so bad if he had new abilities to battle his enemies.

"Where is she?" he asked the night.

He didn't expect an answer, but he received one.

His heart answered and he headed in the direction leaping from the wall and running into the direction of his destiny.

Running across the rooftop of a derelict castle, he soon found an exit below. He opened the trap door and followed a ladder below. Below the castle had some of the finest riches he ever beheld. Had he been taken prisoner and transferred to some faraway land or was this perhaps Valhalla? Had he passed to the afterlife? It would explain the richness of furnishing, the soft fabric beneath his feet, and the strange smells below. He was famished and would see what offerings await him.

As he wound down the elaborate wood staircase, he realized two things – this was not the afterlife, and clearly, this was the home of a magical creature. Fire glowed within glass, but the flame was white. The soft fabric laid a path, perhaps to a throne room. It was not a solid color either and reminded him of a freshly shorn sheep as paused to curl his toes. He followed the smell of meat cooking and something sweet, but he could not make out the exact confection. Voices came from the place of food.

"I'm glad you decided to only face the house in stone, that should cut the labor time down considerably," a woman said.

"Well, I am to please, besides a stone castle with modern amenities wouldn't be authentic," a man replied.

"I suppose you intend to litter the rooftop with stone creatures?" she asked.

Stone creatures? Had Astrid tried her magic on others? Who were these people? Halvor longed for his axe, Angar, and he would strike these *volve* down.

"I don't plan to—"

Another woman screamed, dropping a pan of roasted meat with root vegetables. Halvor found himself face to face with the beings that had captured him.

The man turned. "You're awake. How did that happen?"

"It matters not. I am no longer your prisoner, volve." Grabbing an odd axe off the table, he held it up against his captors.

"For Pete's sake, put down the cleaver." The woman had gotten up from the table and was marching toward him.

"Listen woman, you and Pete need to release me at once."

"Or what?" She placed her hand on her hips and squared off at him.

Pete stepped forward placing a hand on the woman's shoulder. "My heart, you do not know what magic he may possess."

"Magic? I am not some volve! I am human. Listen Pete and Myart, whatever the witch Astrid has involved you in, it is not too late to release me." Halvor pleaded his case in hopes that these powerful beings would find mercy or better yet help him destroy Astrid.

The woman with blond hair and brown eyes looked at him like a herring once caught and then she did the oddest thing. She laughed.

Halvor was so caught off guard he dropped the weapon named Cleaver and then the most humiliating thing happened, his stomach growled. A warrior without a weapon on the field of battle and he is betrayed by his own stomach.

Myart giggled as she spoke. "Libby, if you would be so kind as to retrieve what roast you can for our guest."

The woman named Libby spoke a quiet "Yes, ma'am". Halvor took in the woman's garb and determined her to be a slave or perhaps one of Pete's concubines, deferring to Myart.

Pete stepped forward and spoke, "You can't be serious."

"Ben, he is clearly confused. He does not know where he is, when he is, and he is obviously hungry. I will not let a man starve. I'm sorry your name is…"

"Halvor, son of Sven." He knew not what possessed him to give his name to the enemy. His only logic was that Myart was some sort of enchantress.

"Welcome to our home, Halvor. This is my husband Doctor Benjamin Gunn, not Pete."

"Doctor, a strange name."

"Doctor is my title." The man had reddish brown hair and green eyes. He might be with tribes on the Emerald Isle.

"Like a king."

"No, think of it as our word for healer."

"That is too complicated, I will call you Pete."

Pete looked like he might speak, but Myart spoke first. "And my name is not Myart. It is Laurel."

"Laurel is a tree."

"Yes but it is also my name. And you should call Pete, Ben."

"Why?

"Because that is his name."

Libby was setting a table and Halvor's stomach growled once again.

"Why don't we sit down and we can answer all your questions after you've eaten something."

After eating the best meat Halvor had ever tasted, he drank the clearest of water from an indoor stream called Sink. He was well satisfied and noticed many knives to make his escape. He was plotting as he spoke. "You and your husbands have strange names."

Laurel wrinkled her brow. "I only have Ben as my husband."

"What about Libby, is she not your slave as well?"

Laurel laughed again. "Husband doesn't mean slave."

"What does it mean then?" These beings had strange customs.

"Mate," Ben growled.

Halvor looked once again at them. Ben was attuned to Laurel, Halvor thought because she was a witch, it was far worse. He was in love. "You are not a witch then?"

"I am not." She was holding something back.

"But you are not human like me?"

"We are not. But we mean you know harm."

Before any of them could respond, Halvor felt the thickening of his limbs. "No." He dropped the utensil from his hand and tried to run, but it was too late.

"Ben, what's happening to him?" Laurel rose and was on his side of the table, an earnest look of fear upon her face.

"He's turning to stone." Ben answered as he also came around. "Who has your heart?"

"The witch, Astrid," he forced out his last breath before he witnessed their looks of horror. The Fates were cruel to grant him allies before turning him back to a worthless piece of rock.